WIZARDS' KINGDOM

JARRAK'S DARKNESS

to Cian
The final battle
Rom 2008.

WIZARDS' KINGDOM

JARRAK'S DARKNESS

Colin R Parsons

Illustrated by Derek Jones

ATHENA PRESS
LONDON

ISBN 10-digit: 1 84748 079 9
ISBN 13-digit: 978 1 84748 079 8

First Published 2007 by
ATHENA PRESS
Queen's House, 2 Holly Road
Twickenham TW1 4EG
United Kingdom

Printed for Athena Press

For Kristoffer, Ryan and my wonderful mother

*P*ROLOGUE

*T*he Obelisk of Ashmar has been overthrown and wicked Jarrak – the oldest Catchet of all – has been killed. A large section of Jarrak's army perished in the battle along with Talis, Zendal's long-lost sister.

Crasmont, Mydar and Zendal – the wizards of Wizards' Kingdom – survived unhurt. However, much to their horror, they discovered that another section of Jarrak's army, led by Evilan and the brainwashed Loof, was on its way to overthrow Wizards' Kingdom and seize control of it for ever.

Although overcome with grief for his sister, Zendal knows he must return to his homeland and try to regain his kingdom. Reunited with his stallion, Shim, and with the help of his fellow wizards, Zendal must set off to fight one last time.

Taking supplies from the obelisk and boarding a raft from the jetty, the group of wizards float their way down the Davina River. What lies ahead of them is a total mystery…

A CLOAK OF ICE

There was a jetty behind the tower and tied to it was a raft. It was rectangular in shape and made of solid oak. At one end, a rudder was fixed, comprising a shaft that dipped into the water and a handle that overhung the outer edge. It had sides about a foot high and a rope tethered to the base for support.

Everyone climbed aboard, including Shim, who had to be coaxed into position. Once everything was in place, Mydar took the rudder and, rather nervously, pushed away from the bank with Crasmont's help.

Half a mile or so downriver, a curious thing happened… A colossal sound from behind them caused Mydar and Crasmont to turn. Zendal didn't move a muscle in response; he just stayed silent and still. As if a huge hammer was raining blows upon the mighty obelisk, the building started to crumble. It was as if a giant sculptor had picked on the obelisk for creating his next work of art and was chiselling away at it. Slices of stone peeled away from the top and crashed to the ground with a thunderous boom. The ground trembled from the weight of each blow, sending ripples of disturbance across the landscape. Hairline cracks tore into the stone and gnawed their way down – splitting, chipping and splintering the granite into sizable fragments.

Mydar and Crasmont looked on in absolute

amazement. 'Zendal, Zendal you must see this,' Crasmont cried, but he ignored him.

Like an earthquake had struck, the ground rumbled under the intense pressure, sending a flurry of vibrations into the water and causing a series of waves.

'Hold on, this is going to be rough,' Mydar called to the others.

The first wave soon hit and sent the craft into a slow spin. Another roll of water tossed the small raft counterclockwise.

'Try to hold on,' Mydar shouted, while the raft tilted and swayed in the current. More waves bashed and curled over the sides of the small craft.

Mydar held fast to the rudder as Crasmont held onto Shim's neck as best as he could, gripping the rope with his other hand. Curiously, Zendal didn't move from the spot where he sat. He didn't seem at all fazed by the incident. Another band of water twirled the raft back into its original position and then rolled further off down river. Luckily for the crew, no one had fallen off in the turbulence. One more wave, weaker than the rest, pushed the vessel gently on its way.

The last piece of his empire had fallen. Jarrak was no more and, like him, his dark tower, now a heap of rubble, would crumble to dust and vanish for ever.

'Everyone all right?' Mydar asked with concern, as calm returned and he regained control of the rudder.

'Yes, we're fine, no thanks to Zendal though,' Crasmont mumbled bitterly, gesturing to Mydar and pointing at Zendal, who sat alone on board, his mind in a faraway place.

'What's the matter with him, Crasmont?' Mydar asked.

'I don't know. He was fine after the battle, but when he left the tower I think a part of him stayed there with his sister,' Crasmont said, thinking deeply.

'Do you think he'll snap out of it, Crasmont?'

'I hope so, Mydar. In all the years I've known him, I've never seen him like this before,' Crasmont answered honestly.

★

Time passed slowly as the travellers swept down the Davina River. Out of nowhere, a thick mass of charcoal-grey clouds loomed overhead, concealing every patch of sky and casting a shadow on land and water.

Mydar, the youngest of the wizards, concentrated deeply as he guided the raft as best he could with the rudder. He had never navigated before, but was doing a good job at keeping the raft moving in a straight line. Crasmont was crouching quietly in front of Mydar. He was pondering on what had taken place in the tower earlier that day, and also contemplating what lay ahead. Zendal had been sitting quietly for hours at the head of the raft. He had not moved or uttered a word to anyone. Shim, Zendal's beautiful black stallion, lay on the deck beside his master.

The stallion's hind legs were tucked under his belly and his head rested on his front haunches. The saddle and supply bags filled to the brim were placed to one side. The further they drifted, the quieter it got. Except for the gentle lapping of water at the side of the raft, almost nothing else moved. The landscape around them was unnaturally serene.

Zendal's thoughts were a whirl of dread and confusion. His sister, Talis, a remarkable female wizard, had been killed by the spear of a Kite soldier. They had been reunited after years of separation, but their time together had been so limited.

Yet the battle that had claimed Talis' life had also seen the end of the Catchet warlord, Jarrak. Zendal knew that he should be thankful for his downfall, but the sadness of losing his sister consumed him.

He had retrieved his stallion, Shim, which had been the original aim of the journey, but he hadn't bargained for the rest of it. Kidnapping Shim was only the first part of Jarrak's trick to trap him, his fellow wizards and, most importantly, Loof the Catchet. The whole kidnapping plot was not designed to capture King Zendal, but to bewitch Loof into invading Wizards' Kingdom. Now, with the battle in the obelisk over, the three wizards were lucky to be alive.

Zendal thought with dread and foreboding about the next part of Jarrak's plan. Loof had been brain-washed and had united with the evil warlock Evilan, who had been banished from the Kingdom years earlier. Together, they were on their way to take over Spellock Castle.

Evilan had been defeated before, but this time he had the might of a large army of battle-trained Kites and Seekers. Loof, though always powerful, now had the extra magic instilled in him by Jarrak before he died.

'It's getting very cold, Zendal,' Crasmont commented, tugging his robe tightly around his robust belly. 'It's supposed to be summer!' he added.

'Wha…' Zendal half answered, still deep in thought. He lifted his head and looked round at Crasmont.

'I said, the temperature is dropping rapidly all of a sudden,' Crasmont repeated.

'Is it…? Yes, I suppose it is,' the old wizard answered disinterestedly.

'Since our captivity in that chamber under the obelisk, I don't really know if it should be day or night,' Mydar chipped in casually.

As he spoke, the murky grey sky darkened. First, it sprinkled a light powder of white, which then thickened into a heavy snow blizzard. Fast on its heels came a bitingly cold wind, sealing the landscape in a solid, glistening crust.

'Zendal, what's happening?' Mydar piped up from behind.

'I don't know,' he answered, shaking his head.

'Master, look at the water!' Mydar shouted, pointing his finger at the river.

Zendal stared with glassy eyes at the water. Small chunks of ice were drifting past them, floating along like pieces of a large jigsaw. Bigger portions began connecting all around and forming into a solid block.

'That's very strange,' Zendal uttered, still sounding preoccupied and tugging his hood tightly over his grey hair.

'If this continues at the rate it's going, then the raft won't be able to float,' Mydar said.

At that very moment, and to everyone's horror, they ground to a halt with a thud. The severe conditions had frozen the river solid. Everyone fell forward at the sudden stop. Shim skidded off the raft onto the icy ground. He quickly got up onto all fours and whinnied nervously. Mydar landed heavily on Crasmont and they tumbled to one side.

Zendal righted himself and scampered off the craft, quickly grabbing onto Shim. He then rubbed his hand on Shim's neck and patted him.

'Wow boy, it's all right... it's all right,' he cried, staring the stallion in the eye and stroking the bridge of his nose. This seemed to have the desired calming effect and Shim settled down after a few moments.

To everyone's surprise, the blizzard stopped

suddenly and dissolved into a fine mist. The three warlocks stood like statues, taking in the frozen, desolate wasteland. Everything, as far as the eye could see, glistened in a crystallised desert.

The shadow of Jarrak's evil had descended in the shape of an enchanted winter. With the cold, a twilight effect shrouded the land into semi-light.

'I don't believe this is happening all over again,' Crasmont muttered.

'It's like turning back time,' Mydar chirped up from behind.

Zendal said nothing, but rested his cheek on Shim's long snout and closed his eyes. His savaged mind was too full of anguish and torment to take in the change to his surroundings.

'What should we do, Master?' Crasmont whispered into Zendal's ear.

Zendal turned to his long-time friend and uttered, 'Maybe it's time to give up, eh, old friend?' As he said the words, deep sadness flickered in his glassy eyes.

'Zendal! I don't believe that for a moment. I know you're hurting, but we can't stop now!' Crasmont replied defiantly.

'Master, we can't give up now... We've gone through so much together,' Mydar added, rubbing the old wizard's shoulder.

'It is time to give in, Mydar. Can't you see we're finished? Just accept it.' The king then turned to Crasmont. 'I haven't any fight left, you understand?' He fell silent and walked away a few steps.

His companions turned to one another and stared in astonishment. With heavy hearts, they bowed their heads and let out a long sigh. The two friends stood still; breath escaped their lips like steam from a kettle.

Suddenly, a gust of wind whipped up from nowhere. It blasted Mydar and Crasmont's ears, making them temporarily deaf, and stung Shim's eyes. The stallion stamped his hooves heavily into the ground with disapproval, fighting the sharp pain. A crack appeared underfoot, which spread quickly, cutting jaggedly through the snow.

Soon, another crack appeared, and another, then all three joined, leaving a raft-sized slab of ice with Mydar stranded in the middle. Mydar, not realising the predicament he was in, stayed where he was. The triangular crack widened quickly, separating the chunk he was standing on, so that the whole thing instantly dropped ten feet. Mydar lost his balance, catching the back of his head on the rim of ice on the way down and knocking himself out cold! Crasmont looked on in horror and scampered to the edge.

'Mydar!' Crasmont bellowed. 'Hold on!' But Mydar was oblivious to his calls.

Shim panicked and bolted across the valley. 'Shim! Shim, come back! Come back, I need you!' Crasmont called out helplessly. 'Zendal, help me. Come on, snap out of it. Mydar's in trouble,' he shouted angrily, but to deaf ears.

Zendal's mind was still in turmoil and he didn't know what was going on. He walked a few paces and fell to his knees.

'Zendal! Help me!' Crasmont screamed again – still to no response.

Mydar was lying motionless on the cold, rock-like

surface while the unstable platform beneath him trembled and sank even deeper. The warlock's body rolled over to one side, causing the loose surface to tilt and a gap to form as pieces broke away, revealing a yawning abyss beneath.

'Mydar!' Crasmont screamed helplessly from the top.

Zendal lifted his tired, lined face to the sky, gazing at its grey blandness, oblivious to the danger that Mydar was in. Wisps of cloud danced across the sun's smudged surface, further obscuring its muted glow. The cold air rasped at Zendal's eyes and he became aware of a loud, serene voice, filling his mind.

'Zendal… You can't give up.' The voice swirled around in his head, cutting off all other thoughts.

'Talis, is that you?' he called with a sense of longing.

'Yes… Don't you dare give up now,' Talis commanded.

'But I have no strength left to fight, you must help me,' Zendal bleated.

'You know I cannot. You have the strength of Crasmont and Mydar to help you and they have stayed by your side throughout the darkest of times,' she scolded. 'The kingdom's population needs you to fend off evil.' Her haunting voice swept through his mind. 'Crockledam stands alone to fight the darkness of Jarrak's wrath… Go now and defend your kingdom… You must!'

As the voice of his sister gradually faded away, so did the doubt and grief that had blocked Zendal's path. He snapped out of his inner prison and regained his old spark. The wind died down and Zendal turned to his friends with new determination in his eyes.

'Come on, you two, stop dawdling, we have a king-dom to save,' he said. Then he saw Crasmont peering over the fissure. With one swift movement, Zendal flitted to the edge of the pit and saw his friend sliding into the hole that had materialised at the bottom.

'Mydar, no!' Crasmont shouted in disbelief, reaching down pathetically with his hands.

Zendal realised he had no time to lose. With deep concentration, he levitated over the shaft and floated down to the spot where Mydar's body had just lain. He fell to his knees and squinted into the darkness. From inside his robe he pulled out his amulet and let its sheer brilliance throw a shaft of light into the gloomy depths. A dark object caught his eye – it looked like a dark grey sack hanging in mid-air. Zendal eased him-self a little further in, letting the amulet hang down and do its work. Sure enough, he saw the grey sack was indeed the unconscious body of Mydar, cupped inside a small snow pocket, not moving, but fixed in position. Drawing on the power of the great Orb through his amulet, a pool of light shone down and locked onto Mydar's body. It lifted him up, very gently, through the ice shaft and placed him on the ground next to Crasmont. The chubby wizard produced a blanket from his bag and placed it over his injured friend for warmth.

'Mydar, are you all right?' Crasmont shouted ur-gently, shaking him and kneeling over the stricken wizard.

Mydar began to come round. He blinked open his eyes. Crasmont tilted Mydar's head at an angle and discovered a rather large lump on the back of his head. There was no cut, but a large bruise was already starting to form.

'You'll be fine,' Crasmont said after a swift examination. 'A little dizzy for a while, perhaps, but fine.' He sighed and breathed out a mouthful of cold air.

By this point Zendal had returned to the surface and magically set a fire going.

'I'm fine now,' the young wizard retorted stubbornly, trying to sit up immediately. He was soon put in his place by Zendal.

'Shut up and just take it easy there for a while,' Zendal ordered. 'Crasmont, stop dawdling and make Mydar a warm drink.' Crasmont looked at him in surprise and then did as he was told.

'We'll stay here for a while. Once you've fully regained your strength, we can continue,' the old wizard said, and then let out a long and haunting whistle. Within a few minutes the sleek figure of Shim came trotting back into camp.

Crasmont made a bowl of hot stew and gave a share to Mydar and Zendal, keeping some for himself. He gave Shim some carrots and cabbage and they all settled down for a rest while Mydar recovered. The shock took its toll and, feeling warm and comfortable, Mydar drifted off into slumber.

'We have a huge task ahead of us, Zendal,' Crasmont commented, gazing into the flickering flames of the campfire.

'We have to find our way out of this place before we can even contemplate anything else,' Zendal replied grimly. 'Let's get some sleep, old friend, so we can all be ready for whatever crosses our path next.'

★

It was some hours before Mydar was awake again and feeling stronger. Zendal stood up, stretched his arms and gave out a yawn.

'How are you feeling now, Mydar?' Crasmont asked. 'Any better?'

Mydar got up and winced, gritting his teeth. He rubbed his tired eyes and gently cupped his hand to the back of his skull. The throbbing lump had subsided to half its size, but was still very sore to the touch. He still felt a bit dizzy, but didn't let on.

'Yes, a lot better thanks. I do have a slight headache though,' he said. With that, Shim trundled over to the young wizard, put out his tongue and licked the sore spot.

'Don't worry, boy, I don't blame you for this. It was just one of those things,' Mydar said, reaching round to stroke Shim's mane.

'Enough of this nonsense! Are we ready to take our kingdom back?' the king asked with excitement.

'*Yes!*' the two wizards responded, realising their old friend had returned in mind and body. Even Shim whinnied in approval.

'Now, to business.' Zendal surveyed the land with new eyes. With everything powdered over in white, it was difficult to plot a course. To his extreme left lay a forest, picturesque in its winter shroud, but unfamiliar territory. Beyond that, a range of needle-sharp mountains could be seen. To his right were the flatlands and valleys leading back to Ashmar.

'This way, I think,' he said, seeming to choose a direction at random, and away he went. Zendal burst into stride with renewed vigour and confidence.

'Come along, we haven't all day!' His words echoed in his wake as his two friends looked at each other and shook their heads in disbelief; it was as if nothing had changed; things were finally back to normal.

Without letting on to his companions, Zendal smiled to himself and breathed in deeply. *Thank you, Talis*, he said in his thoughts.

WHISPERS

*H*ours had passed since the wizards had left their stranded wooden craft on the frozen bank. They headed wearily across this new land. A few miles ahead, the flat landscape flowed uphill and was swallowed by woodland. This forest seemed strangely close at first, as they shuffled along the white virgin snow, but every mile gained didn't seem to bring them any nearer.

Each step crunched and cracked underfoot as the fresh fall compacted. It was difficult to know if it was day or night in the twilight world they now inhabited. Whether it was the sun or moon smudged behind the dense layers of cloud, they just couldn't see! The only piece of luck in their favour was the fact that the bleached snowfall reflected the meagre glow from the sky, giving a little more light to the proceedings.

'My word, Zendal, look at that!' Crasmont panted, his eyes rounded in awe.

'I know what you mean; very strange indeed,' the older wizard said, staring in the same direction, a gulp of cold steam pouring from his open mouth as he spoke.

'Wow!' was all Mydar could muster as he tilted back his head, almost cricking his neck, straining to see the tops of the trees.

The closer they came to the monster trees of the

forest glade, the more they realised just how enormous they really were. Each colossal frame easily outweighed and overshadowed the greenery of Dursley Tops (one of the wooded areas in Wizards' Kingdom). Even the illumination of the snow, reflecting light from the sky, didn't make a dent in the shaded gloom of the forest. The gaping holes leading inside were like the deepest and darkest of nightmares.

'We're all tired, let's see if there's shelter inside so we can rest a while,' Zendal announced. Shim gave a snort and shook his head in disapproval.

'Come now, Shim, what's the matter, boy? Would I lead you into any danger?' Zendal coaxed, patting the stallion's broad neck.

'I don't know, Zendal, I have a weird feeling about this place.' Mydar's face revealed his anxiety.

Zendal was taken aback by his youngest companion's reluctant approach. Normally Mydar was the first to explore new and exciting places, but this mysterious forest seemed to unnerve him. Looming in the background, his other fellow warlock, Crasmont, looked a little agitated too.

'What's the matter with you two? We've been to much scarier places than this in the past,' Zendal said with surprise. 'Well, I'm going in; it's bound to be a little more sheltered in there than out here in the elements,' he said, turning to proceed, with Shim closely behind. Crasmont and Mydar looked at each other. The younger wizard gave an apprehensive stare at the other and nodded.

'Come on,' he said. 'We've got to go.'

Crasmont sighed heavily, closed his eyes and shook

his head as he walked in gingerly.

With their king in front, both wizards followed in his footsteps and soon they were all inside – in almost complete darkness. Overhead, the broad arms of the branches interlocked, forming a great natural roof, which acted as a solid barrier that the winter conditions could not penetrate. The ground was hard and dry and each wizard groped along helplessly. Zendal shuddered as he felt the hot steam from his stallion's nostrils billowing over his right shoulder. They released their amulets and the blue stones quickly emitted a small source of light, glowing dimly in the large expanse. Zendal leaned over and picked up a short, thick, discarded branch which lay in his path. Almost immediately he was knocked over as the other two walked straight into him.

'You fools,' he spouted sheepishly, realising it was mostly his fault.

'Oops, sorry,' the two warlocks uttered in unison, covering their mouths and trying not to laugh.

Zendal grasped the stick and wrapped one end in a strip of material he produced from his robe. He held out his index finger to the gauze and concentrated…

First his finger glowed orange, then bright yellow. A small spark of energy appeared at the tip, then burst from the end and touched the dry wood, exploding it into life. The rich golden glow cast a dome of light, penetrating the immediate shadows that limited their vision and giving up the secrets of the forest. It looked like a different world. A place where, if you were not careful, you could lose yourself for ever!

One particular hollow, beneath a root caught

Zendal's attention; there was enough room inside to house the three of them and the stallion with ease.

'That's where we'll rest for now...' He smiled, pleased with himself.

'And eat,' Crasmont interrupted hungrily. 'We must eat,' he repeated.

'Good grief,' Mydar sighed, 'you'll never change.'

'Yes, yes Crasmont – and eat,' Zendal confirmed as Crasmont settled down to make a warm broth.

Soon, inside the hollow of the giant tree root, mouth-watering odours of stewed meat and vegetables wafted in the air – the food they'd taken from the obelisk's kitchens. Swirling, light grey smoke twisted and rose up through the hollow tree trunk, escaping through various rotted holes in its bark. The warmth of the fire and the fulfilling meal eased their troubles for a while, letting them forget the task ahead. Cupfuls of wine were poured from the pouch – red wine also taken from the obelisk – and each of them was ready for sleep. From a fiery yellow blaze, to a gentle amber glow, the campfire slowly burned away, deep into the night.

★

The tranquil wasteland trembled violently. An enormous brown stain spread relentlessly across the snowy plains, marching out of Ashmar and across the border into the Cascoo desert. The fresh snow crunched under the enormous feet of the Seeker soldier ranks. Thousands of dwarf-like Seekers trudged on in military order. Steam poured from their wide, pig-like nostrils; their beady, black eyes were deep and menacing. Each figure grunted and growled in unison.

Seeker-drawn wagons creaked and jolted along the icy ground. Inside each one were supplies of food and drink to nourish the hungry hordes. Ear-shattering screeching from above pierced the sky at a million decibels, as thousands of bird creatures swooped ever onward. Their eyes glistened like lava-filled pools, their razor-sharp teeth and claws glinted their worth as deadly weapons. Loof and Evilan were leading the movement; the full weight of Jarrak's soldiers trailed behind their new masters.

The troops came to a complete stop as Loof raised his hand. They were standing at the edge of a huge precipice: a wall in the desert with a steep drop and a wide fissure to the other side. Loof winced for a moment, gripped his stomach and gave a twisted satisfied smile. Recovering quickly, he turned to Evilan and declared that they would have to make some kind of bridge. With the wagons and half the army on foot, they needed to find a path across. The Kite army would obviously have no problem in flying over the gap.

'What about magic? It would be easier and quicker with magic,' Evilan urged.

'No, we'll need all our magical strength to keep the troops in line – now and in battle,' he answered.

Loof quickly gestured to one of his Kite aides. Evilan looked on as he whispered something and soon the creature was winging its way to one of the wagons. The Kite soldier, with the help of a few others, fished inside the cart and picked out coils of sturdy rope. Chirping to one another, a few more Kites joined in and grabbed stakes and hammers from another wagon. Snorting Seekers, standing nearby, looked on, completely mystified as to the Kites' intentions. Armed with a complete make-shift bridge, the Kites dropped the four coils of rope at the feet of Loof and Evilan. Four solid stakes were also placed on the ground, each five foot long and a foot thick. The stakes were spaced out in a perfectly-measured sequence.

Evilan called over a group of Seekers and they immediately started to hammer the stakes into the snow-clad ground. With their huge, muscled torsos, they easily pummelled the four wooden pegs into place. They drove the stakes into the earth to a depth of three and a half feet, leaving a foot and a half of wood protruding from the ground to attach the rope to.

A large group of Kites appeared, grabbed the ends of the ropes, and picked up the hammers. Four more stakes were brought by more Kites and carried over to the other side of the ravine. Taking longer than their muscle-bound counterparts, the Kites nevertheless eventually succeeded in driving the stakes into the ground. They then attached the ends of the ropes to the stakes, completing the next stage of the improvised bridge.

A great rumble silenced the mutterings of the ranks. As instructed by Evilan, more Seekers had appeared with another wagon. This time it contained a huge reel of sheeted canvas material. It was tethered together with tough criss-cross strapping. It took six Seekers to roll it off and set it in front of the rope structure. Ingeniously, one Seeker soldier slowly rolled the canvas carpet onto the wide path of the suspended ropes. Simultaneously, Kites, armed with strong leather thread, wove the strands through the eyelets at the edge of the material. They easily dipped and darted along the length of the bridge in swarms, like bees in a hive.

Once the crossing was ready, Loof gave the command for the troops to make their way across with the wagons. The first cart rolled along the canvas 'hammock', pulled by two Seekers. It worked perfectly, the canvas taking the full strain with ease. So he sent another across.

This procedure of moving thousands of Seeker dwarfs across a huge ravine took hours to complete and slowed the pace of the army right down. Everyone made it across, except for one or two wagons which had rolled off, but Loof and Evilan weren't concerned about them – it was a success!

★

Later in the day, after marching for a long spell, Loof's concentration was interrupted. A single Kite glided down, hovered gently at his shoulder and squawked into his ear. A dwarf Seeker waddled up to Evilan's side and also grunted a message to its master. He stared back into the pig-like face and hissed a reply as the animal cowered.

'They need to rest,' Evilan conveyed miserably to his companion.

'So do the Kites,' Loof told Evilan in disgust. 'We have no time.'

'They are no good to us if they can't fight, we need a strong and alert army to conquer Spellock Castle,' Evilan reasoned, his eyes fierce and sharp.

'We'll camp here for the night then,' Loof muttered.

The two soldiers waited patiently for an answer. Loof turned to the Kite and gave the order in the birds' language. Evilan gave the Seeker the same information. The messengers relayed the order to the ranks and campfires sprang up like measles on the open ground.

A tent was erected, staked to the frozen ground with iron pegs beaten home by two Seekers, its coloured canvas bellowing and flapping in the night breeze. The two leaders entered the tent to discuss their plans. Loof settled on one side of a square, make-shift table and Evilan sat opposite. Food and wine were placed in front of the two leaders and the Seeker servant retreated outside after his duty was fulfilled.

Evilan and Loof sat in silence, staring deeply at each other. Loof uttered the first words. His usual friendly smile and warm expression were lost as he operated deep under the influence of Jarrak's evil spell. A dark and fearless malevolence commanded his form now and nothing remained of the old Loof.

'I felt a sharp pain earlier, just as we entered the Great Wall. I'm sure some force has come to an end,' Loof revealed. 'I have no fear now of anything following us – the wizards are no more.' He grinned widely back at Evilan.

'Pity, I would have liked one last battle with those weak fools… Now there is only the pitiful resistance they've left behind. No matter; a swift and rich victory awaits us then.' Evilan scowled, toasting a vessel of wine to his companion.

'Yes, we'll march into Wizards' Kingdom and easily take it for ourselves,' Loof concluded, swigging a mouthful of wine.

'Yes, we shall rule for ever,' Evilan replied with delight, a spark of excitement rippling through his body. *I shall crush you, Loof, as soon as I have my chance*, Evilan thought wickedly.

I will rule with you as my servant, Loof's inner mind declared.

They toasted each other once more and eventually retired for the night.

★

An enormous disturbance shattered the quiet of sleep; it emanated from deep in the camp. A ferocious fight had broken out between the Seekers and Kites. Four Kites had attacked a Seeker from all sides and his companions had joined in the war of breeds. The sounds of jeering and goading filled the cold harsh air as the fight exploded. Tearing, slashing, screeching and grunting took centre stage. The two sides were fighting viciously when, suddenly, it was all over. Out of the blue, ten Seekers exploded into dust and fourteen Kites were obliterated on the spot. Heads quickly turned to Evilan and Loof and saw the anger in their eyes. Loof shouted, 'Anyone else want the same?'

Deep hatred filled each creature's eyes – vast loathing tempered with fear. There came no reply.

★

'Mydar... Mydar...' Whispers bled through the air. Mydar's black hair flopped to one side and his eyes flicked open as he lifted his head from the make-shift pillow. He took short sharp puffs of air and eagerly scanned the immediate area. Visibility was poor; the only light came from the red-orange glow of the fire's dying embers. Mydar lurched onto his elbows and looked all around.

To his left, the dim light revealed the robed back-side of Crasmont's snorting torso. To the right, Zendal stayed silent, only jerking in his sleep at intervals. Still drowsy, the young sorcerer slumped back into sleep.

'Mydar... Mydar... Wake up!'

This time he jerked bolt upright.

'Wha... What's going on?' he slurred.

'Come, I am waiting for you.' The voice was little more than a whisper. He couldn't even make out if it came from a male or female. Mydar climbed to his feet, adjusted his robe and wandered outside the tree cave.

'Over here, come!' the voice continued, its tone hypnotically magnetic.

'Who are you? What do you want with me?' Mydar called back in return. He eased his amulet out of his robe and into the open, letting the bright stone guide him in the dark wooded cavern.

'Where are you taking me?' he called, now in a stronger, thicker voice. He noticed, as he strode along, a sweet aroma – a soothing fragrance, pleasing to the nose. His feet shuffled through the loose bark and twigs announcing his arrival to his tormentor…

★

In the midst of fighting an enormous snow monster, Crasmont jumped in his dreams and kicked Zendal in the head. The old wizard rolled over, rubbing his sore noggin.

'Crasmont, you idiot!' he bellowed and kicked the dumpy wizard squarely on the butt. The chubby wizard immediately woke up, eyes blazing.

'What did you do that for?' Crasmont snorted moodily.

'Never mind, never mind… Where's Mydar?' Zendal quizzed, noticing his companion's absence, while still rubbing the back of his head.

Crasmont rubbed his own tender backside. 'I don't know. He was here when I went to sleep, I'm sure he was…' he mumbled, trying to remember. By this time, Shim had woken and stood up.

'Come on, we must find him,' Zendal announced, bounding outside and grabbing a burning branch from the fire on his way.

Outside it was as black as tar. Zendal held out his flaming torch as he steadily manoeuvred himself along the darkened tunnels of the forest.

'Wait for me, Zendal,' Crasmont called from behind, peering here and there as he went. He and Shim followed the yellow tint of Zendal's light deep into the wood.

'What a wonderful smell, Shim,' Crasmont said, sniffing the air and stumbling along to keep up with his companion.

It wasn't long before they came to a clearing. In the centre, sitting crouched on a rock, was Mydar. The scent was at its strongest here and Zendal stopped. There was no one else, just Mydar sitting motionless.

'There you are! What are you doing here?' the old wizard asked, sweeping his gaze from side to side.

Mydar craned his neck and stared deeply at Zendal. 'You have always got to be the one in charge haven't you?' he spewed in disgust.

Crasmont had only just appeared with the stallion and heard what Mydar said. 'Mydar, I think our king deserves a little more respect than that, don't you?' he said in a damning tone.

'Mind your own business, Dumpy, this is between me and him,' the young warlock said, pointing his finger toward Zendal.

'Who do you think you are, you young upstart?' Zendal bellowed back in retaliation.

'I should be in charge, not an aging, worn-out wizard like you, Zendal,' Mydar said, continuing his onslaught.

'Why you—' Before Zendal could answer he was cut short by Crasmont.

'Shut up, Zendal. I am the one who should be king of our land, not you or you, Mydar, you snivelling tree grub.' Zendal turned to see Crasmont's eyes brimming with hatred. Suddenly Mydar was blasted through the air, landing on one side of the clearing. Zendal was blasted to the other side, his fire stick flying out of his hand.

Shim raised himself onto his hind legs and whinnied nervously. Mydar was fast on his feet and sent powerful bolts of electricity in Crasmont's direction. His magic hit home and sent the warlock spinning sideways uncontrollably. Zendal then emerged and fired magical fingers of light, hitting Mydar's right flank and sending him sprawling into a bush.

Crasmont burst forward out of nowhere and attacked Zendal from above, lifting him off his feet and bouncing him down a slope. All three returned once more to continue the fight and aimed power bolts directly at one another. They moved in with hands raised, attacking at every opportunity. An unremitting stream of solid blue light flowed from each wizard's body, slowly draining each of their power. Shim reared up and kicked out violently. Crasmont, Mydar and Zendal broke off the attack, tumbling into submission. Once recovered, they all stood up and grasped their freshly-aching limbs.

'What was that for, Shim?' Mydar asked innocently, staring at the steed and rubbing his bruised backside.

'I have a headache,' Crasmont complained, resting both his hands on his forehead.

'I think we have been shown the secrets of this forest. It took our weaknesses and used them against us. Luckily for us, Shim understood this. Now, let's get out of here, before we try to kill each other again!' Zendal said, picking up his torch, which was still burning. He made his way back to the tree cave to retrieve the rest of his belongings.

'Well done, boy.' Zendal's voice echoed through the forest as he patted Shim's neck.

'Where do we go now, Zendal?' Crasmont asked earnestly.

'We make our way back through this forest. Come on, you two,' he said and walked on with his stallion trotting proudly by his side.

'Zendal, what are you saying? We go back through there? We were close to death only a few minutes ago,' Crasmont said without understanding his master's reasoning.

'I don't understand either, Master, why put us back in the path of danger?' Mydar demanded.

'This is the biggest forest we have ever seen. How

long would it take us to walk round it?' he asked them. 'We know what to expect now and time is of the essence.'

His companions both nodded, unable to counteract this reasoning. All talked out, they followed Zendal deep into the dark mysteries of the quiet wood.

THE ONLY WAY THROUGH

E very snap and rustle begged the wizards' attention in the ominous gloom.

'What was that?' Crasmont called out nervously.

'Hey, Spooky, calm down or you'll have us all on edge,' Mydar jeered. Zendal just darted his gaze from side to side and continued cautiously.

Darkness was overwhelming inside the giant forest, but things slowly began to change. The monstrous trees started to fan out, allowing light to filter through. The air felt sharp and heavy on the lungs. The poor excuse for morning brought back the harsh reality of why they were there. The sky was still a swirl of muggy cloud, endlessly concealing what the true weather should be. Inside the heart of the forest, the winter was kept out by the vast network of branches, but out here the boughs were whitened in a thick covering of snow. A cold chill blew past the wizards making them shudder.

'Is this going to be the outlook for eternity?' Crasmont commented, frowning and shaking his head.

'No it's not!' Zendal burst back defiantly. 'We will change all this back, Crasmont. That is why we are here now. Do you understand?' His eyes sparked with defiance.

'Yes, Zendal,' Crasmont answered sheepishly and the conversation ended there. Mydar just looked on in silent thought.

They left the dense trees of the giant forest and made their way through an area of thick bushes. Inside the forest it was quite easy to manoeuvre between the giant stumps, but here things were different. Branches reached out like clawed hands, tugging and tearing at the travellers. To make things worse, a powdery mist rolled in and saturated the undergrowth. The mist engulfed everything in its path and the wizards were finding it increasingly difficult to see. Shim snorted loudly and shook his mane.

'Easy boy, there's nothing to worry about. It's just cold mist,' Zendal said, comforting his steed. 'This is getting hopeless,' Zendal muttered, clawing his way through the brush.

'Master, let me see what's ahead. I'll climb this tree; maybe there's better visibility up there,' Mydar said. With a nod from his master, he began to climb.

'Be careful, Mydar,' Crasmont said, but as Mydar was young and fit he was already halfway up. There were so many long and twisted limbs it was quite easy to ascend. Finally, he stopped and peered through the haze.

'What can you see?' Zendal called from below.

'It's just thick mist coming in fast, Master. Everywhere looks the same.'

'Come down then.' And soon Mydar was back on the ground.

The fog continued to thicken and its wispy dance coloured everything a shade of grey. It wasn't just difficult to see; now it was impossible! Mydar put his hand in front of his face and, until it touched his nose, he would not have known it was there. Still the almost human limbs of the bushes grabbed and pulled at them.

'Zendal, Mydar, I can't see you!' Crasmont's voice shrieked through the gloom. Zendal stopped in his tracks.

'Stay close, Crasmont. Mydar, are you all right?' Zendal hollered.

'Yes… I'm right by your side,' the voice of the young warlock replied.

'Crasmont, hold onto Shim's tail. Mydar, you do the same. It sounds a little ridiculous, but humour me.'

Shim shuddered slightly with the two fists tugging his tail, but Zendal calmed him. The stallion trampled through the bush nervously, led by Zendal. Behind him the two wizards did their best to hold on.

'Mydar, I've never experienced… such a… deep, choking mist,' Crasmont conveyed while trying to negotiate a rather clingy branch.

'Yes, this is not the normal drifting fog that just floats and disappears,' Mydar replied dismally.

Shim suddenly lurched forward and stumbled. He whinnied and snorted, yanking his tail out of the wizards' grasp!

'Shim, what is it boy?' Mydar called in concern.

'Aaargh…' Zendal's voice exploded from dead ahead.

'Zendal! Zendal, are you all right?' Crasmont shrieked, surging forward with Mydar at his side.

The mist was too dense for them to see much, but they found Shim. He was snorting frantically and shaking his head, while digging his hooves into the icy ground. His grip was less than safe and he struggled to hold his ground.

'Zendal… Zendal… Where are you, old man?' Crasmont called, tracing his hand along Shim's back, along the nape of his neck, over his ears and down his snout. Mydar's hand was already ahead of his companion's and he felt the strap that was clenched between Shim's teeth. His fingers finally grasped Zendal's hand. It was cold and gripped tightly around the leather strap.

'Zendal, grab my arm,' Mydar shouted.

'I cannot let go, I'm barely holding on as it is,' Zendal shrieked.

'Zendal, I have your sleeve.' Crasmont joined in and the two sorcerers pulled on the old king's arm as hard as they could. He began to lift towards the edge and they almost had him. Suddenly, Shim's hooves slipped. He slid forwards, making Crasmont and Mydar hurtle towards the edge over which Zendal had fallen. Frantically digging in his hind hooves, Shim slid on, desperately trying to regain his grip.

'Hold on, Crasmont!' Mydar screamed.

'I can't… I can't,' he bellowed back.

With that, Mydar, Crasmont and Shim slid over the edge to join Zendal. All four tumbled and slid down, down, down! Crasmont and Mydar were still defiantly holding onto Zendal's sleeve and still gripping Shim's muzzle. They rolled and bumped from side to side, unable to see where they were headed.

'What… is… this?' Mydar exclaimed, trying to stay upright.

'It's not a pit… we would have fallen in… vertically… and landed by… by now,' Zendal rasped at them, sliding at a rate of knots.

Their flight picked up speed and the cold wind rushed past their frozen ears. Mydar turned upside down on the smooth, icy surface and glided at a ferocious pace, picking up more speed.

Crasmont was on his back and could feel the hot, steaming breath from Shim's nostrils next to his own face.

'Wow... you need some mint herbs, boy,' Crasmont blurted, spinning upside down.

The steep slope suddenly divided into channels. The split sent the sprawling group in different directions, each one on a separate toboggan run. Their echoing shouts bounded off into the bleached grey mist.

'I know what this is...' Zendal shouted from a distance.

'Well?' Mydar gasped impatiently, zooming like a rocket with no control whatsoever.

'We're on a frozen waterfa—' And Zendal's voice vanished.

Everyone realised too late as they tipped over the

edge of the final drop and surged down the waterfall, crashlanding at the bottom. The impact of their landing took its toll on a thinner part of the glacial surface, cracking open a sizable chunk. Blinding mist was the least of their problems now! They were sucked under into a freezing dark world, with no escape. Bubbling water deafened them as they were submerged.

Zendal tried to surface, desperately clawing his way upwards. He could feel no one around him, so he kicked out, pushing up through the water. Gradually, the old warlock ascended, only to find his fingertips grinding on a ceiling of ice. He was trapped under the frozen lake! He pushed further along, his lungs gasping for air, until his numbed hand felt an open space – a gap in the ice! With a last burst of energy, Zendal exploded through the water's surface and gulped in mouthfuls of chilled air. He choked and heaved, coughed and spluttered, his lungs feeling like trampled pigs' bladders. His chest pained him deeply and his limbs were all but frozen stiff. Slowly, he regained some sort of composure, despite the freezing temperatures, and trained his mind on the others. His teeth chattered violently as he trod water and felt his way along.

It was more than just a gap; the further he moved, he realised he was in a large hole in the ice. He shivered, clenched his teeth and called out.

'C-Cras-mm-ont.' He gulped at the air.

'My-dar… Sh-i-m…' This was all he could utter as the pressure on his chest and lungs squeezed ever tighter. He began to fade; his mind fuddled and his eyes rolled. He drew on all his wizardly powers of meditation to stay conscious, but it failed him. Like a dying campfire, all thought drifted away...

Then, suddenly, his whole body jerked violently downwards. Again, he felt the tug on his ankle. He reached down and grasped a hand in the depths. This brought new life into the old warlock and also brought Crasmont to the surface. In a frantic *splosh,* Crasmont broke through and gulped in air as Zendal had. Soon, behind him, rose Shim, snorting and shaking his head and wildly cavorting around, trying to stay afloat. Just behind him, the remaining wizard, Mydar, exploded onto the scene. All four were treading water, creating icy waves. The ice was closing in and each wizard was barely staying afloat. Their stiffened arms and legs were tiring.

'Are... we... all... here?' Zendal said, barely getting the words to escape through his chattering teeth. The answer came in a two muffled groans.

With one last effort of his mind, Zendal penetrated Crasmont and Mydar's inner thoughts. 'Use your amulets and break the ice,' he commanded.

'I... I can't,' came the defeated reply from both Mydar and Crasmont.

'You... must.' Zendal's thoughts trickled inside Mydar and Crasmont's subconscious. Like a gentle tide, Zendal's calm, superior voice seeped through. A new strength welled up inside them.

'Come, Mydar, you must try. Crasmont, you must force your mind.'

For a moment nothing happened, just the gentle lapping of the lake and the crackle of new ice forming... Then three brilliant blue lights fused as one, exploding from the stones.

A beam, as strong as the sun bleaching the dawn, was released into the ice. The power of the wizards carved through the crystallised barrier and melted a pathway around them, lighting up the scenery like a beacon. A twilight world of colour replaced the deep-cloaked grey. A cold winter breeze frosted their faces, but the warmth of their medallions eased life back into their veins. This sudden charge of heat gave way to a soft dreamy sensation, taking its toll on their exhausted bodies. Too weak to clamber out of the sub-zero temperatures, they all slipped under the water once more. Before Zendal closed his eyes for the last time, he saw two huge beady eyes peering back at him…

★

Loof stopped in his stride. A disturbance among his army had caught his attention. There was excitement in the ranks as Seekers and Kites alike eagerly pointed to the distant skies. A luminous shaft of electric blue light filtered through the gloom of winter and stood prominent for all to see, before gently evaporating. Loof felt a twang of pain deep inside his stomach and gripped his abdomen. He knew the wizards were alive and a strange sensation of guilt flittered through his mind. For a moment his eyes widened and confusion cast a shadow of doubt. All too soon the feeling passed. Evil once more washed over him and a stern, determined force regained its place.

'What's wrong, Loof, you having doubts?' Evilan sneered.

'Are you feeling threatened, Evilan? There are no doubts here,' Loof replied, turning to his counterpart. They stared at each other and Evilan smirked and turned away.

★

The sound of a crackling fire brought Crasmont round. He opened his eyes and stared contentedly at the yellowy dancing flames and spitting sap. The chill of the lake was a distant memory. His clothes were dry, the fire hot and a fantastic smell wafted from a black pot hanging over the flames. He gingerly sat up, rubbed his aching sides and smiled. A long, rumbling groan came from the pit of his stomach, waking Mydar, who was lying next to the hungry wizard.

'I might have known,' Mydar said, lifting himself onto his elbows and rubbing his tired eyes; but Crasmont was preoccupied. Crasmont wasn't looking at the fire anymore, but beyond it. Mydar followed his gaze. There, seated a little further from the fire, was a group of shadowy figures…

By this time Zendal had regained consciousness and now joined the proceedings. 'Where are we?' he whispered. This seemed to be the obvious question.

Shattering the quiet, a long, trumpeting snort blasted from behind.

'Quiet boy!' Zendal hushed his steed, gently feeling behind and rubbing his hand smoothly down the bridge of Shim's long, wide snout. Never for a moment did he take his eyes off the strange people gathered on the other side of the campfire.

There were about thirty of them, most of them sitting, but some standing in the glow of the roaring fire. They all looked very similar. They were tall, slight creatures, with pale, narrow faces – almost blending in with the snowy surroundings. One thing that really stood out, though, was their eyes. They had huge round eyes, like dinner plates, with little black peas for pupils. Their mouths were wide slits just above the lower jaw. To literally top things off, their hair was bushy and pure white.

'Who are they?' Mydar said, scratching his cheek.

'I don't know, Mydar, but if it wasn't for them we would certainly have perished,' Crasmont answered, continuing to look with an unbroken stare.

'They remind me a little of the Rock People of the Shallow Water,' Mydar said. The Rock People were a strange race of creatures that had helped the wizards to fight Evilan's army in the past.

'Let's go over there and thank them for the good deed they have done and be on our way.' Mydar had made up his mind and was ready to move.

'No!' Zendal cried out.

'What is it, Zendal?' The two wizards recoiled.

'My amulet… it's gone,' he replied bitterly.

At this, Crasmont and Mydar urgently felt inside their robes and gave out a similar sigh.

'We have to go over there and get them back,' the old king blasted defiantly.

'I agree, Zendal, but with a certain amount of sensitivity; they did save our lives,' Crasmont added.

All three wizards stood and Shim rolled onto his

legs and quickly righted himself. The colour of day was still winter grey and as the wizards stood above the fire the cold air cut into their faces. The strange creatures now also stood and the wizards felt like midgets in their presence. They reluctantly strolled towards them and stopped a couple of feet away.

Zendal boldly took two steps forward. 'Thank you for your help,' he said, stretching out his hand in friendship.

The creatures flinched and quickly circled the band of wizards, frowning in retaliation, their dish-like eyes narrowing. The wizards hadn't noticed previously, but these strange people were carrying thin straps that looped over the shoulder. They surrounded the un-suspecting warlocks and stood fast. The straps suddenly flashed a luminous red and pulsed.

The wizards were transfixed, waiting to see what would happen next. As quickly as they had moved into position, the creatures removed the glowing loops and interlinked each one until a red circular barrier surrounded the wizards.

'We mean you no harm,' Crasmont offered nervously, trying to support Zendal's efforts.

Mydar lurched forward only to be stopped by the old king as Shim stamped his hooves into the crusty snow.

'No, Mydar,' Zendal whispered from the corner of his mouth, grabbing Mydar's wrist.

'You must come with us.' One warrior, slightly taller than the rest, uttered the words threateningly, without breaking the red glowing band.

'We cannot. We have an important journey to

continue,' Zendal asserted. In unison, the creatures stepped forward one step, reducing the size of the pulsing ring. Mydar reacted instinctively. He broke free of Zendal's grasp and dashed straight ahead.

'No! Mydar, no!' Crasmont shouted helplessly as Zendal gritted his teeth in silence.

The younger wizard made contact with the barrier and was thrown back as if being hit by a lightning bolt. He landed at Zendal's feet and opened his eyes to see Zendal's disgusted expression.

'You will come with us!' their leader said forcibly.

Zendal thought for a moment. Seeing that they didn't have much choice without the power of their amulets he paused, looked at Crasmont and then down at Mydar.

'All right, but you must give us back our amulets,' Zendal said.

'No, the amulets will be returned after you have spoken to Lord Faal of the Demonites. Now sit and enjoy our food.' The leader's forceful tone left Zendal no room for protest. Zendal looked at Crasmont and Mydar and soothed his stallion.

'We have little to say in this matter,' Zendal admitted. 'What was that stupid move you made, you fool? Mydar, you could have killed us all,' Zendal chided.

'But—'

'No buts this time, Mydar. Listen to Zendal,' Crasmont said, patting his companion on the shoulder. Mydar shook his head in defiance, but relented.

The Demonites dropped their guard. Once the circle was broken the wizards returned to their place at the front of the fire and the Demonites slipped their weapons back over their shoulders. Hot food was brought and served to the prisoners, to the delight of Crasmont. A small group of Demonites joined them and settled by the fire.

'Who are you?' the Demonite leader asked.

'I am Zendal and these are my friends Crasmont and Mydar. Sorry about his outburst, but he was defending me.' Mydar blinked and lowered his head. 'With whom do I speak?' Zendal asked politely.

'I am Reed of the Demonite people. This is Clay and Fleet,' Reed explained, his two companions nodding. 'We have enemies in these parts known as Scalers and we have to be careful whom we deal with.' The Demonite commander looked at them suspiciously.

'We are not your enemy, Reed, we merely wish to pass and be on our way.' Zendal continued, 'We thank you for saving us; we would definitely have perished in that lake otherwise. We must get back to Wizards' Kingdom.' This statement didn't seem to spark any recognition in the creature.

'Once Lord Faal has seen you and given me permission to release you, then you can have your amulets back and be on your way,' Reed stated. 'I will let you continue your meal and then we must move on.'

Before Zendal had a chance to ask any more questions, the three Demonites stood and rejoined their group.

'Well we're stuck for a while,' Crasmont said, finishing off the last of his food.

'Master, I'm sorry for—'

Zendal raised his hand in interruption. 'I understand, Mydar. I would have done the same in your position,' he said with a smile.

AMBUSH

fter the meal, everything was packed away and the fire was doused. The smoke billowed high into the cold air creating swirling shapes. Crasmont coughed a dry cough from deep down in his throat, choking on the pungent air. They left camp as soon as they were ready. The cold chill of the enchanted winter lingered like an unwanted guest. The ground was uneven and rock solid. *We must have been brought here from the lake because the waterfall is nowhere in sight*, Zendal thought.

The wizards and their beautiful black stallion were put at the centre point of the Demonite army formation. They weren't shoved, hustled or forced, just gently positioned into place. However, they weren't allowed to move out of position and were still refused access to their amulets. At the spearhead of the movement were Reed (the leader), Clay and Fleet. Just behind them were their followers, about six of them, marching in front of the prisoners. The wizards were flanked on each side by three more stern-looking Demonite soldiers. At the rear was another group of eight soldiers and behind them was a small wagon. It was a two-wheeled cart with two poles jutting out from the main frame and was being pulled by two more soldiers. These were also flanked by five more of the creatures. Trailing behind everyone came another two Demonites, bringing the total to thirty-two. *A well-disciplined and well-organised body of creatures*, Mydar thought, impressed.

Zendal said little, but took a lot in. He walked at the same pace as everyone else, but in total silence. Crasmont and Mydar knew this as a sign that the old sorcerer's mind was working overtime. In many a grave situation in the past, Zendal had saved them with a well-calculated risk. He just needed time to think.

In the distance, on the outer fringes of the white desert, stood a guard of tall trees, heavily frosted with a milky crest. Mightily overshadowing this regimental cluster was a range of mountains – huge chunks of jagged granite standing proud and foreboding.

'This is taking us miles out of our way, I'm sure of it,' Mydar pointed out begrudgingly, in a low tone. He shrugged his shoulders and moved on slowly, shuffling his feet to show his disapproval.

'There's not a lot we can do at the moment, Mydar. We'll have our chance at some stage,' the chubby sorcerer asserted and looked at Zendal. 'Zendal... Zendal, what are you thinking? What's going on?' Crasmont chirped noisily.

'Will you keep quiet, you're attracting attention,' Zendal snapped back.

Mydar rolled his eyes at Crasmont patronisingly and Crasmont scrunched up his nose in retaliation, like a child.

'Master, that wagon...' Mydar leaned across excitedly, whispering through his fingers, while pretending to rub his nose.

'Yes, I've been thinking that too,' Zendal said,

gazing longingly at the wooden cart.

'Oh, you mean the amulets,' Crasmont burst out in realisation. His two companions closed their eyes and shook their heads in disbelief.

'Oops,' Crasmont said, touching his finger to his lips, but the Demonites were too absorbed in scanning the area to listen.

'I think the cold air has gone to his brain and frozen it,' the young wizard mocked. 'I didn't notice that wagon at the camp site, though.'

'It must have been hidden behind the undergrowth somewhere,' Zendal surmised. Something caught Zendal's attention and he flicked his gaze all around.

'What is it, Zendal?' Crasmont asked, staring into the old warlock's eyes.

'Something's wrong; these creatures can sense it and so can I,' Zendal exclaimed boldly.

Gusting winds formed from out of nowhere. They blasted through the ranks like sand through a sieve, sucking up clouds of white powder on their travels. A mini-blizzard took place, instantly making visibility impossible.

Shouts rang out from the Demonite soldiers as they produced scarves to protect their faces from the biting cold and the blast of snow crystals. The wizards pulled up their hoods to prevent the icy clouds from stinging their eyes. Shim reared nervously and Zendal tried to calm him. Reed called to his men to group closer together, his voice partly lost in the ensuing *whoosh* of wind.

'Just beyond the ridge... there is shelter... we make for that point,' he called out.

The wizards were then herded along through the sweeping storm, but it was getting increasingly difficult for the Demonites to keep control. Curtains of white flakes rushed towards them.

'Zendal, now would be a good time,' Mydar called out in all the confusion, but Zendal was having problems of his own trying to calm his stallion. Mydar pulled Crasmont to one side. Crasmont closed his eyes and positioned his ear to Mydar's mouth, listening intently.

'The trailer,' he called. 'Let's get our stuff.' He made a break for it, then suddenly stopped dead!

'Wha… What are you doing, Mydar? We haven't time to stop now!' Crasmont exclaimed, flushed with impatience.

'Look ahead, Crasmont. What is that?' By now Mydar was rubbing his eyes, screwing them up, trying to make out something, then rubbing his eyes again. Turbulent gusts of air were creating a vast wall of powdered snow, but beyond the veil were dark patterns. More shapes loomed from the perimeter, moving and changing shape. Echoed screeches resounded from all sides mixed with the howling, whistling winds. Crasmont, confused by all the movement, squinted into the dusty snow blast.

'What are they?' he screamed nervously, peering through the snow.

'Scalers!' a voice burst out.

This brought on a sudden, knee-jerk reaction and the Demonites resumed their circular formation, exactly the same as when they had surrounded the wizards. This time, however, they were facing outwards, not in.

Once again, the Demonites interlinked the straps that they carried on their shoulders and formed a red ring. Its powerful brilliance produced a pinkish tinge that reflected off the swirling snow flakes. As if controlled by evil itself, the storm began to subside a little, leaving a clearer view of the enemy advance. The full impact of the ambush soon revealed itself. The strange creatures, called Scalers, were advancing from beyond the ridge.

'What are they? Where are they coming from?' Crasmont questioned in confusion and fear.

At first they appeared as a vast band of elderly people, moving forward in no particular order, ambling on foot. Each one was hunched almost double. The hind legs were human-like, but bowed and with splayed toes. A deep mass of short, tangled, matted hair covered their whole shabby-looking bodies. Their arms were thick at the shoulder and thin at the wrist; each of their clawed hands hung limply and appeared harmless and weak. Their upper and lower jaws were filled to the hilt with razor-sharp teeth, like the rocky base of a cliff. The creatures' heads were oblong with a protruding snout and they sniffed and grunted like boars. Their movement was slow and awkward, reminding Mydar of Loof's Seeker foot soldiers. But there were so many of them – around three hundred – more than enough to penetrate the Demonite defence. The echoed grunting became louder – their form of communication. Closer and closer they came, spreading out and surrounding the make-shift Demonite stronghold. Zendal became alarmed and felt helpless at the situation.

'Reed,' Zendal called out, but the leader was standing with his comrades, linked together by the power straps. Zendal scurried over to him while Crasmont, Mydar and Shim looked on.

'Reed, you must give our amulets back, we can help you,' Zendal pleaded.

'I cannot; you have to prove yourselves to Lord Faal,' he barked defiantly as the first wave of creatures hit the barrier. Zendal pleaded again, but Reed ignored him and concentrated on the job at hand. Mydar, meanwhile, had lurched onto the unprotected cart and feverishly clawed through the contents searching for the amulets. Screams of pain filled the chilled air as bodies were thrown back by the ringed power surge and twenty or so Scalers collapsed to the ground. Unperturbed by this, more Scalers came forward, unceremoniously stepping over their battered comrades. In an almost trance-like state they heaved against the Demonite defence and were cast aside in the same fashion as the others. Zendal moved back and rejoined his companions, biting his lip in annoyance.

'Master, they aren't there,' Mydar confessed bitterly. 'I've gone through the cart from top to bottom, but nothing!'

'If not there, then where are they?' Zendal raged impatiently.

'They may not need our help after all, Zendal,' Crasmont said, watching the third attack of Scalers collapse.

Again the air was filled with grunting and screaming and the smell of burned flesh wafted around in a horrible stench. Another impact and the Scalers were down to two thirds of their original number, but Zendal could sense the power ring fading. A huge pile of Scalers were strewn about on the ground. The snow had churned to mud, but the continued onslaught was proving too much. The bright red magical circle of defence began to dim.

'Let us help you; give us our amulets back,' Zendal demanded once more.

'No!' Reed bellowed in defiance, turning to Zendal with fear in his eyes.

★

Quietly and nervously the little Snow Fawn nibbled away at the shoots that were poking through the frozen crust. Her black eyes glistened like windows in the snow's reflected light. She dipped and tugged at a particularly stubborn patch of tasty clover. Unbeknown to her, a pair of excited eyes peered through the branches of a Clanny bush. The boy's breath heaved in hushed, sharp bursts and his heart throbbed so loudly he couldn't hear properly. Tentatively, his hand shaking, he lifted his bow and, not taking his eyes off the fawn for one moment, he gently slotted an arrow into place. The fawn was far too busy wrestling with the shrubbery to notice the intruder. Taut and true, Treela aimed the arrow straight at the animal's belly. The young hunter's fingers began to strain and tremble slightly. A bead of sweat trickled down his forehead, along the line of his nose and dropped onto the arrow shaft.

Up popped the fawn's head and, instantly, off she darted in a panic. Treela, bemused and positively annoyed at his loss, lunged from his hiding place and gave a pathetic chase, to no avail. His prize had flown. He stopped in mid-flow, flicked his head to his left and dived for cover in a patch of undergrowth.

With a mouth full of snow he spluttered, spat and gently clawed the branches apart to view the scene. His eyes widened to the full and his mouth dropped open.

'Good grief,' he whispered and shrank further back into hiding.

A resounding low hum rumbled the ground. Half a mile away, just crossing the boundary of Wizards' Kingdom, was the biggest army of Seekers and Kites Treela had ever seen. He remembered seeing pictures of the creatures in scrolls that King Zendal had once shown him, but this was real. He scrambled away, keeping low to the ground until he was positive he couldn't be seen anymore. Jumping to his feet, and moving as fast as his young legs could carry him, he sped homeward to Spellock Castle to inform Crockledam.

★

The situation was hopeless. At least two hundred Scalers were still attacking. The power of the red ring had paled; the huge bursts of energy that had kept the Scalers at bay were now only giving a mild electric shock.

'Reed, you must give us the amulets or we will all perish,' Zendal demanded.

The Demonite leader thought for a moment, but there was no time to ponder and a spark of decision filled his eyes. 'All right, you can have the amulets,' he relented.

It was too late, though. Two of the Demonite defenders fell to the ground, screaming, with Scalers clawing and tearing at them in a savage attack. Mydar flexed his magical power to conjure up his bow and Crasmont summoned his magic power whip, but without the precious amulets the weapons would not come.

Zendal moved forward in a bid to intervene, but without warning the Scalers whimpered like scolded dogs as, miraculously, their robust bodies were pounded to the ground. Shim instinctively reared and crushed the creatures under his powerful hooves, his eyes wild and glassy, his nostrils steaming and flared in the burst of adrenalin. The old wizard reached out and stroked the creature.

'Well done, boy,' he whispered in his ear. This seemed to ease the stallion's tensed form.

'Reconnect the ring of power!' Reed shouted immediately.

The Demonites that had been attacked stood back up and regained their position in the circle. Once linked back together, the fading power ring somehow burst back into its former glory. To everyone's surprise, new squeals of pain and turmoil sounded above the cries of the Scalers on the front line. The terrifying, piercing eyes of the Scaler enemy filled with confusion and despair.

Almost drained of fight, Reed looked on in joy. The three wizards were as confused as the enemy. A new super brilliance of red beamed through the fog-chilled battle line. Scalers began to retreat in different directions, trying to find an escape route.

'What's happening, Zendal?' Crasmont called out. Reed's face filled with a deep smile and he breathed a thankful sigh.

'What does this mean, Reed? Why are you suddenly so calm?' Zendal asked. Suddenly, he saw in the clearing another army; this time it was a rescue party. A hundred or so Demonite people filtered out from the same direction from which the Scalers had emerged.

What was left of the devilish Scaler army dispersed back into hiding to the cheers of Reed and his small pocket of soldiers. Once the battleground was safe, both groups of Demonites replaced their weapons.

Reed, Clay and Fleet stepped forward and embraced their rescuers' leader.

'Nailor, we are so glad you came when you did.' Reed smiled excitedly and patted his friend's back.

'What? You three couldn't defeat these few stragglers on your own?' he sneered, looking at the piles of barbarians scattered over the land.

'You spoilt all the fun. We could have finished this lot on our own,' came the sarcastic reply from Clay and Fleet.

'What do we have here?' Nailor studied the three travellers and the beautiful stallion that stood behind Reed's men. The three wizards peered back in silence. Outnumbered by these new creatures, Zendal knew it was futile to try and escape, especially as they still didn't have their amulets to defend themselves. Using their own power without the amulets, and against such a powerful people, would certainly be very foolish, Zendal thought, mulling over the problem. As quickly as they could, they must meet the Demonite master and sort things out. Then they could be back on their way to sort their own problems – and time was running out, he could feel it!

'They are from a place called Wizards' Kingdom and are making their way back there after Lord Faal has seen them,' Reed conveyed.

'I have heard something of that place. I recall a wizard many years ago called Veltzeg; he travelled this land once and met Lord Faal,' Nailor said with a spark of recollection.

Mydar tensed and almost stepped forward, but Zendal gripped his arm and squeezed it gently, using his authority to command the situation.

'Yes, King Veltzeg once ruled Wizards' Kingdom, but he died a few years ago. I am now king,' Zendal proclaimed proudly.

'Then you won't mind meeting our lord, so let us take you there without any more interruptions.' Nailor stopped the conversation short. He turned and called his men, who gathered in readiness.

'Please follow us.' Reed quickly walked on.

'We almost had our amulets back,' Crasmont complained.

'Let's attack now, Master, we can take them,' Mydar hissed, raising his fists and clenching his teeth.

'We are outnumbered, Mydar, as you can see. We must follow and wait,' Zendal answered wisely.

'Zendal, we haven't the time to waste, as you well know,' Crasmont said, sympathising with Mydar.

'Look, I know as much as anyone that we haven't the time to waste. My kingdom is under threat and may already have been taken by Loof and Evilan,' he replied. 'I want to go as badly as you, but we are stuck until we get our amulets back.' He broke off the conversation and walked on silently, as Shim rubbed his snout against Zendal's shoulder.

The Demonites reformed and headed through the winter landscape as the haze of swirling snow danced in mini tornados around them. By now, there weren't any Scalers in sight and, with a whole body of Demonites, it didn't look as if there would be any more trouble.

Within two hours they had entered a low flatland. On the outskirts were groups of snow-covered trees, but in one area to their right the yellow glow of a fire flickered against the brilliant white of the winter scene. On closer inspection, igloo-type huts could be seen – cunningly placed so that they lay hidden in the wilderness and drew no attention to the homestead. One such igloo was much larger and grander than the rest. As Zendal looked on, it was obvious to him that this must be Lord Faal's.

The other make-shift homes were simple and basic in structure. As they moved closer in, they saw that the larger igloo was triangular in shape. In contrast to the others, it had beautiful animal carvings set into its smooth, ice fascia. Just beyond this igloo, the fire was located.

In the middle of the village, people had gathered in a welcoming party. The army had arrived home. The three wizards and the stallion were asked to sit on the far side of the fire, opposite and facing the ice palace. They were served with food and told to wait. The villagers, made up of women and children, didn't speak to the new strangers in their camp, but just stared at them. Finally, after an hour or so of waiting, all the mystery vanished as Lord Faal majestically joined the proceedings.

SIEGE

Taking care not to be spotted by the overhead Kite patrols, Treela kept below the treeline, dodging and weaving through the undergrowth, only stopping to regain his breath. Then he continued on, sinking into the deep snow and sliding on the icier ground. He knew that the enemy wasn't far behind.

He was a young boy of about twelve and very frightened. As he sprinted, his heart slammed hard against his chest. He was agile and could run for miles at a time. The army behind was slow in its progress and Treela didn't realise how quickly he'd fled. He finally reached Spellock Castle and burst through the passageways, heading directly to Crockledam.

'The army is coming... The army is...' He keeled over, breathless and faint.

'Settle down there, young lad.' Crockledam's deep gravel tone oozed calmness.

'B-b-but the... army is... coming, Crockledam... I... I've seen it.' Treela just about managed to heave the words from his mouth.

'The Orb sees all. There is nothing to fear, lad – not at this moment, anyway.' Crockledam eased himself up, called the townsfolk and sent servants to alert the people. The Orb whirled into action and things began to change.

★

Evilan raised his hand as a signal to stop the troops. Loof peered through the foggy grey veil and laid eyes on the beauty of Spellock Castle. Nestled in a beautiful natural setting and frosted with a winter glaze it looked magnificent. A thick layer of white snow covered the normally smooth grass that surrounded the base of the castle. This vision of splendour and romantic beauty was about to change; in its place would come violence, bloodshed and death.

'Come on, Loof, we have no time to stop and stare. Let's take it, here and now,' Evilan hissed.

'What do you see, Evilan?' the Catchet asked coolly.

'What do you mean? It's Spellock and it's unguarded – empty, even,' he replied with angry eyes and gritted teeth.

'It's completely quiet – no movement of people or creatures of any kind,' Loof said suspiciously.

'But it doesn't matter, they have no defence against us. We know there are no wizards there; the villagers are no match for our army,' he retorted.

'Where is Crockledam? He was left in charge,' Loof said.

'Perhaps he has fled with the others and abandoned the castle with his tail between his legs.' The dark wizard smirked.

'We will proceed, but with caution,' Loof advised.

'Very well, but I see no point,' Evilan contested, his mind swirling with mutiny.

The Catchet called five Kites to his side and

motioned them to fly within spitting distance of the walls and then report back with what they had seen. All five took flight and quickly soared through the thickening grey skies towards the ancient building. Clicking in communication with one another, they hovered over the outer walls. It was still; the whitened towers stood defensive and strong as they had done for a thousand years. There were no footprints of any kind to give clues to any movement. The Kites' wings flapped frantically as they swooped a little further in. Two of them descended and landed in the courtyard, disturbing the dusty surface as their wings settled. Their yellow eyes glared at one another; they scurried along and leaped up onto the balcony in their search for any sign of life. The others hovered, watching every move from above.

Evilan and Loof looked on in anticipation from the outer perimeter.

'Come on, Loof, there obviously isn't anyone there or they would have found them by now... We're wasting valuable time,' Evilan ranted impatiently.

'We wait until we know,' Loof answered without even turning towards his annoying companion.

Satisfied there was no threat, the winged creatures rejoined the others and all five returned to Loof, conveying their message.

Loof looked at Evilan and signalled an order to march on and breach the stronghold. Slowly and cautiously they closed in. The Kites, knowing there was no threat inside the empty building, decided to continue on foot rather than fly. The rest of the troops surged like a black band of death across the frozen land.

The dark force encircled the castle like a noose tightening round a poor soul's throat. Loof felt a twinge of regret, but quickly shrugged it off. The closer they got, the bigger the old monument became. Its gigantic gates were left open invitingly. A broad smile lit the usually cold features of Evilan's face. Deep pleasure filled his whole being. *At last, Spellock is mine once more*, he thought. Now within thirty feet of the gates, Loof signalled the army to stop.

'What are you doing?' Evilan questioned in a rather disgruntled and impatient manner.

'There is something strange here,' Loof said, his eyes narrowing. He frowned with a flicker of suspicion in his eyes.

'We thought that no one here was expecting us,' Loof explained with uncertainty.

'Yes… so?'

'Then why is the castle not filled with its inhabitants, carrying on with their normal duties?' Loof queried, gazing at the ground and shaking his bald head in puzzlement.

'We've been through this, Loof. That's why we sent in the Kites… Or are you having second thoughts… Are you afraid, because if you are…' He peered deeply into the Catchet's eyes. 'I can lead this army as I did before, you know,' he said, not moving his steely stare from Loof's face.

'Don't even think of it, Evilan,' Loof retorted, but suddenly stopped as something caught his attention.

Some of the Seeker soldiers grunted with excitement and Evilan turned to see what had disturbed them. They were looking upwards and Loof joined in, following their line of vision. There, on the outer wall, staring down with arms raised high, was the enormous frame of the troll, Crockledam. He appeared calm, his great dish-sized eyes openly devouring his audience.

Above his head, raised high, he held a huge boulder, which rested in his shovel-like palms. For a split second Crockledam and Loof locked eyes. The huge troll's eyes widened even more. He then realised that Loof was now his enemy and not the friend that had left on the journey with his wizard companions. With anger in his heart, he heaved the mighty rock directly at the army. At the same time, the castle gates began to move and gradually ground to a close.

The two evil leaders had no time to urge the army forward as the boulder fell down. The massive rock, accelerated by gravity, came crashing into twenty or so Seekers and Kites, killing them in a snap. Shrieks of horror and disorientation came from the surrounding creatures.

'What a pathetic attempt to ward us off, you snivelling oaf,' Evilan snarled at the troll; but with the impact came another surprise. The ground beneath began to crack along a widening seam, branching off every which way. Like a fragile eggshell, the ground disintegrated under them, spilling snow crystals into the abyss. Evilan's smug smile suddenly faded. He turned pale as he and Loof realised what was happening. Where the ground was breaking, the fissure that opened revealed a huge expanse of water. Cries of panic boomed all around as the Kites and Seekers were sucked down without mercy. Further and further back the ground rippled and split under the weight of the pig-like soldiers. The Kites spontaneously lifted into flight to avoid the perilous waters and instinctively made for attack over the castle walls. Some Seekers tried to grasp the legs of the flying beasts in a feeble attempt to escape drowning. As the Kites shook them off and gained height, the winter sky filled with a dreadful hail… a deadly flurry… of arrows.

The slim spears sliced through the enemy hordes. With no chance to reorganise and defend their ranks, one by one the Kites were hit and plummeted to their death. Deluge after deluge of missiles smashed them out of the sky into fine brown dust.

Booming helplessly from below, Loof's voice

penetrated the squeals of defeat. 'Go back! Quickly, get back!' he bellowed as he and Evilan were drawn into the panic and confusion.

Seekers thrashed about helplessly in the icy lake, their eyes filled with panic and dread. They couldn't swim and each one clawed and clung onto their comrades in an effort to stay afloat.

Huge chunks of ice separated, creating a vast gulf of water around the castle. The Seeker soldiers at the edge of the bank had got the message to withdraw, but behind them the others pushed on, herding more of their companions into the freezing depths. Loof managed to clamber back to the outer bank and scramble onto solid ground, as did Evilan.

'Loof hates water,' he screamed in temper as he wrenched himself to his feet. 'Back, you fools, back!' he shouted in anger.

Gradually, the first battle came to an end. The last of the victims that had fallen into the water sank and perished below the surface. The remaining enemy soldiers scampered off in retreat, with one or two more being picked off in a final arrow attack.

'I don't understand it, there's never been a moat surrounding that castle that I can remember,' Evilan spluttered angrily, coughing up half the lake.

'Obviously it's been added in Zendal's absence, as a deterrent,' Loof replied with distaste, stunned at being outmanoeuvred by his enemy.

'Let's go again, right now!' Evilan demanded in defiance.

'No, we must think this through. Who knows what they have in store.' He walked off and pondered for a while, then flicked around with a look of sheer hate.

'What is it Loof?' Evilan shouted impatiently.

Loof padded forward and stood within touching distance, lifted his head and stared into the inky black eyes of his comrade.

'Crockledam has my amulet,' he announced. 'I gave it to him as I left for Ashmar.'

'So we are not just dealing with a few peasants, here. We are dealing with a troll with the power of Wizards' Kingdom. Well that makes me feel much better... you idiot!' he ranted disrespectfully.

'Be careful, Evilan, I won't tell you again,' Loof retorted, his eyes burning with anger and his whole body tensed.

'You don't frighten me, Loof, so don't threaten me either,' Evilan spat. 'You are no match for my power and don't you forget it.' They locked each other in a piercing stare for a few moments, before breaking off and walking away in different directions.

★

Inside Spellock Castle Crockledam gathered Zendal's people.

'We have won this time, but things will get worse. We must be ready for another attack,' the troll conveyed seriously. 'Now I must consult the great Orb and try to reach our king.'

Crockledam entered the throne room and concentrated his mind to the all-powerful Orb. He knelt there for a while with the amulet Loof had given him; there was no response. Either the wizards were dead or they were separated from their power amulets. Now he realised there was only one thing to do. With or without his sorcerer friends to help him, he must defend Spellock Castle. Maybe one day they would come back and reclaim it.

Crockledam remembered that Zendal had left him with one spell, just in case he didn't return. With the amulet gripped in the palm of his large right hand, he went through the instructions that had been so carefully relayed to him. He uttered the words in a low, soothing, gravelly tone, again and again.

The dark blue liquid inside the glass ball began to swirl; faster and faster it revolved. Its hypnotic motion almost sucked Crockledam's mind into its glassy depths. Then a fantastic power shaft burst through. A white liquid spray seeped through the corridors and passageways of Spellock. It flowed from room to room, filling the castle with a pale, milk-like substance.

Within seconds it had washed its way into a complete circular barrier, engulfing the whole of Spellock Castle. It then transformed itself into an invisible outer wall, surrounding the castle grounds and rising way up to the very top of the towers. Crockledam sighed; it had happened just as Zendal had said, but for how long would it protect them?

★

About a mile or so from the great castle the two evil leaders gathered their army. Loof regained his wits and called upon a large flank of about six hundred Kites to approach him.

'What's going on?' Evilan probed suspiciously as he entered the proceedings.

'You know what to do. Enter the castle, wait for my signal and kill everything you see,' the powerful little Catchet announced, his beady eyes blazing with fire. In a deafening display of violently flapping wings, the Kites made for the sky.

Evilan had his own plan and called a thousand Seeker troops to his command. He gave his orders and they reacted at once.

The Kites were already on their way, soaring through the grey half-light. Below, on the ground, the Seekers pummelled the short distance to the castle in heavy force.

Overhead, deafening wailing and piercing screeching whipped every Kite into an attacking frenzy. Six hundred flocking birds shook the very foundations of Spellock. Like a humongous swarm of irate bees, the creatures flew within the outer boundary of the ancient building. They flew upwards, spreading out, and encircled the perimeter wall. Once they were in position they looked down on the courtyard and saw the population flooding out into the castle grounds. The people jeered and goaded the Kites to attack, but the birds held their position. Below them were the icy waters that had already taken a quarter of their number.

The Kites quietened down until just the sound of rasping wings could be heard. The foot soldiers surrounded the building and halted on the edge of the moat. Hovering in readiness, the Kites' wide yellow eyes were almost hypnotic. A mixed feeling of lust for battle and fear of the glistening water tormented the flying soldiers – for Kites, like their Seeker counterparts, could not swim.

Working together, Loof and Evilan pooled their minds as one in a spell of interwoven dark magic. The rippling water seemed to still and stiffen. At one stage it resembled a gigantic mirror as it solidified into its original form of solid ground. With nothing to stop them now, the Seekers were given the order to attack. The sky creatures were also released to fight. Premature cries of victory showered from above and pig-like grunts gushed in support from below. The din echoed across the plains for miles and the onslaught began.

However, as soon as the soldiers hit the castle's invisible barrier, they instantly exploded into tiny brown dust. The Kites' lightning-quick advance sent them straight into oblivion and all that was left was a dark brown haze. The Seekers met the same fate. Evilan and Loof looked on in utter rage.

Through the rusty fog of disintegrated bodies a figure loomed ominously into sight. As the dust settled and visibility improved, high up on one of the castle's mighty towers stood the tall, broad body of

Crockledam the troll. He knew Loof could see him and a huge grin filled his boulder-sized face. His steely gaze cut into Loof's heart like a knife. The Catchet, though, was too quick for the troll and flicked up his right arm, sending a bolt of pure crystal energy from his slender little finger. It cut through the protective barrier and the impact was absolute. In the time it took Crockledam to realise what had happened, the troll hit the ground with a huge crunch. The impact sent a shiver through the corridors and doorways as the spell melted away, leaving Spellock's inhabitants without any protection from the enemy.

Loof's eyes danced with excitement. Knowing the last defence was gone, the two evil wizards made straight for the gates of Spellock and burst through. Their remaining army peeled away and let the leaders past. A new zeal overwhelmed the Catchet as he crossed the border into his new realm.

Everyone inside was in total panic. They tried to defend the castle, but it was no good. Evilan burst through the courtyard and cast an old but vicious spell. Once more the population stopped in its tracks. Rock replaced life as the people turned into statues and stood motionless, silently welcoming the victorious invaders.

I now have everything I need, and this time I intend to keep it! Evilan concealed his evil thoughts.

First port of call was the throne room and they quickly made for the treasured throne. Like children fighting over a toy, they squabbled among each other until Evilan slid in front.

'I am now in command,' he said with satisfaction, 'but you may be my second in command.' He curled his lip in a snigger.

'You are under some strange delusion, Evilan. Jarrak wanted me to take the kingdom, as you know very well,' Loof retorted.

'You are out of your mind if you think I will give up my right to you,' Evilan rasped.

Loof said nothing and walked away. He walked out to the spot where Crockledam lay. He knelt over the troll's body, then turned and walked back into the throne room.

'You have finally come to your senses have you?' Evilan questioned.

The wizard stood up, but Loof had other ideas and instantly conjured a spell. Evilan had no time to react and he too was turned to stone like the others. The dark wizard's hard eyes were trained on the Catchet's neck. Just before he solidified, his eyes had rested upon the amulet that hung there…

A new form of power had taken over the castle. Spellock now belonged to the tiny but very clever Catchet and no one was going to take it away from him.

THE CHALLENGE

*L*ord Faal, the great leader, graced the centre of the square. Tall, like his subjects, he turned and faced the wizards. The fire crackled and snapped, sparking purple-blue flashes inside the deep yellow-orange flames. Grey wisps of smoke danced and escaped into the faded charcoal sky. The rippling heat of the fire distorted the Demonite Lord's features as he announced his presence. His eyes were wild and round; his stance firm and true with an air of elegance. Unlike the ordinary folk around him, he distinguished himself with regal attire. Fastened around his slim neck was a strip of flat brown leather. Coloured stones were fixed onto it in a perfect sequence: two lines of three on each side and a large, green, triangular stone dead centre. In between each glassy bead were symbols, elegantly carved into the leather strap. The wizards tried to work out what the symbols meant, but neither of them recognised the language. A medium-sized polished stone was also set into Lord Faal's forehead. As he surveyed the strangers, it glinted in the firelight.

'We are—' Zendal began.

'They claim they are wizards travelling through on a special journey, Your Lordship,' Reed said, before Zendal had time to explain himself. The wizard looked at him in muted disgust.

'No one passes through my land: wizard, peasant or any creature,' Lord Faal blasted. The three wise warlocks sitting before him could see his audience cower at his words.

'He is a very powerful leader,' Crasmont whispered to Zendal from the corner of his mouth.

'We are no threat to your people, Your Lordship. We mean no harm,' Zendal announced with authority, but modifying his tone slightly for the sake of diplomacy.

'Reed, explain the rules of this court,' Lord Faal commanded and then turned away, standing with his back to the wizards.

'Court, what court? This is not a—' Zendal spluttered, but was drowned out by the next proclamation, spoken by Lord Faal's second in command.

'Anyone crossing through this land without per-mission has to take The Challenge,' Reed explained. King Zendal's eyes narrowed and he thought for a moment.

'What sort of challenge?' Zendal questioned curiously, weighing up what may be to their advantage.

'Challenge? We have no time for any challenges,' Crasmont interrupted abruptly.

'Quiet Crasmont, let them explain first. Please con-tinue.' Zendal cast a friendly eye and a nod to Lord Faal and glared sternly at Crasmont. He was trying to work out his next move and Crasmont wasn't making it any easier.

Reed waited for quiet and continued with his speech. 'Lord Faal will challenge one of you to a duel of skill and magic… If you win, you can be on your way; but if you lose, you can never leave this place and will be Lord Faal's servants for ever more,' Reed explained and then stepped back a pace, bowing his head in respect.

'Then I accept the challenge,' the old warlock said, volunteering himself.

'Silence! He will be the one,' Lord Faal said, turning and pointing directly at the young warlock, Mydar. Mydar's eyes bulged and his cheeks reddened.

'But I… I…' he stammered as his mouth dried and his jaw dropped. He looked at Zendal in utter bewilderment and Zendal looked totally surprised.

'This is nonsense. I have already agreed to challenge you, not Mydar,' Zendal retaliated sternly, throwing his hands up in protest.

'Silence, I have made my decision and my decision is final,' the Demonite leader whipped back in a temper. 'Do not question my authority!' He placed his hands on his hips and stared solidly, his disk-like eyes burning like torches.

'Zendal, we can't let Mydar take this challenge,' Crasmont protested.

'Don't you think I know that, Crasmont? Let me think,' Zendal said, rubbing his temples feverishly. But it was too late, the competition had already begun.

'Step forward, young Mydar.' Lord Faal beckoned the young wizard forth. Zendal reached out and squeezed Mydar's shoulder in support. Shaking slightly and still stunned by Lord Faal's decision, Mydar gathered his wits and pooled all his courage.

On the outer edge of the circle, the Demonite people sat down cross-legged and formed a solid ring.

Zendal and Crasmont sat either side of their companion. Behind them, Shim, silent as ever, stood vigilant.

A small pile of rocks was brought into the circle and placed to Mydar's right, next to the fire, between the two contestants.

'I will start the proceedings,' Lord Faal announced with relish and rubbed his hands in satisfaction.

'Hey, hold on a minute! What are we meant to be doing?' Mydar asked impatiently, baffled by the mystery of the event.

'Hold your tongue and I will explain,' Faal rasped, annoyed at the outburst. 'We must move one or more of these stones without touching them.'

'I must have my amulet then,' Mydar demanded, folding his arms in defiance.

'Amulet? Of what amulet do you speak? Why was I not told?' Faal raged and turned his head towards Reed. The servant gulped a large mouthful of air and scuttled to his master's side.

'A thousand apologies, Your Lordship, it slipped my mind,' Reed answered sheepishly and called for the amulets to be brought forward. A single Demonite came to the leader and plucked the necklaces from a small pouch on his waistband. Faal examined them for a moment, smiled, and handed them back to the trustee, who replaced them in his belt.

'In order to beat me in this challenge, you must do it without the aid of your amulet. If you do defeat me, then the amulets are yours and the three of you can be on your way.' Once Faal had presented the terms he gazed back into the fearful face of Mydar.

'But… but without my amulet, I can't…' Mydar mumbled, terrified at the fate awaiting him and his friends. Once more he felt Zendal's hand on his shoulder. Crasmont gripped his other shoulder, allowing him to gain a little stability. Everyone fell silent again.

'I shall begin,' Faal said confidently.

Mydar, don't worry. You have the help of Crasmont and I. Our combined power will win this fight.

Zendal's message flooded Mydar's head. He felt warmth and a flood of confidence sooth him.

'Are you ready, boy? You look a little preoccupied,' Lord Faal gloated.

The leader of the Demonites closed his eyes in concentration. The symbols engraved into the leather on his necklace suddenly beamed into life, glowing and reflecting in unison with the coloured stones next to them. Mydar knew something was coming to a peak when the red gem on Faal's brow also began to emit light. The next moment it was glowing as brightly as the necklace. Of the five stones that lay in the pile, the uppermost one began to shudder. Then it wobbled and began to lift, very slowly, above the other dormant stones. While this was happening, the coloured stones around Lord Faal's neck burst into new life. Mydar sat open-mouthed, wanting to speak, but not daring to.

'Hold on, this is not fair,' Zendal protested.

The rock fell back down with a *whack,* bounced off the others and rolled to one side. Lord Faal blinked, opened his eyes and sat up in a temper. Some of the Demonite soldiers moved forward to attack, but Faal shook his head at them and waved them away.

'You dare to break my concentration to cheat in this competition!' he shouted angrily.

'Do you think it fair that you can use your magic stones and we can't use ours,' Zendal retaliated with a condescending air. 'What is fair for one is fair for all,' Zendal declared. Lord Faal paused for a moment and then his face lifted into a smile.

'Very well, Zendal. It's only fair, I suppose.' Lord Faal relented and closed his eyes once more. The same stone began to shake and shudder. It lifted up slowly and hung in space. This time the leader's necklace stayed dim and didn't emit any power.

The rock not only floated over the flames of the fire but, as an added test of skill, it began to spin like a top. A few oohs and aahs came from the audience. The stone stopped revolving and floated majestically back to its place on the pile. Lord Faal opened his eyes and peered back at Mydar, relishing the nervous look on his opponent's face.

It was now Mydar's turn and he could feel the pressure on his next move.

Concentrate your mind, Mydar. Think of the stones as grains of sand, not a as a pile of rocks. Zendal penetrated the young warlock's mind.

Mydar closed his eyes tightly and pictured what his master had told him. A moment or so went by and nothing happened.

Relax, Mydar, relax... Zendal urged.

Mydar listened to the wisdom of his friend and eased up slightly. The same rock came to life and began to levitate. It didn't spin like it had before with Lord Faal's magic, but it did hang in the air until Mydar replaced it on the pile.

'Well done, young warlock, I am impressed,' Lord Faal congratulated his challenger.

Mydar relaxed a little, knowing he had the strength of his two friends to help him.

'Ah, I see you are what you say you are – a wizard in the first degree,' the Demonite leader complimented his opponent. Mydar just sat there and smiled.

'I now have a different challenge. Let's see how you deal with this.' As Faal said the words, Mydar's smile vanished.

'I thought that was it. You didn't mention there would be more,' Mydar curtly replied.

'I didn't say there wouldn't either,' retorted the Demonite with a smug grin and then stood up. Mydar could now see the full height of his frame. Lord Faal bent over, reached out his hand and, with his index finger, drew two lines in the snow. He drew one in front of the young wizard, who looked on in curiosity, and the other just in front of the spot where he had been sitting.

The snow was compact, but a powdery layer still existed on the surface. Without a word, Lord Faal moved to the pile of rocks, picked up the one they had used before and placed it halfway between the lines.

'What does this mean, Your lordship?' Mydar asked impatiently.

'This is more of a test for you, rather than a challenge for both of us,' Faal answered enigmatically.

'A test for me…' Mydar repeated blankly.

'The stone represents freedom for you and your friends. We will both lift the stone using our minds,' he explained. 'The first person to push the rock over the opponent's line wins – simple, don't you think?' Mydar heard Lord Faal's words, but suspected that anything to do with this crafty leader was far from simple.

'Is this the last test?' Mydar asked earnestly.

'Yes, this will decide whether you are powerful enough to beat me or not.'

Suddenly, things changed. Mydar was ready to continue when two guards appeared from behind and removed their straps. They looped them over Crasmont and Zendal's heads. Immediately Mydar's mind cleared of his companions' thoughts; he was on his own now!

'You will do this deed with your own magic,' Lord Faal said, revealing his true cunning.

'You knew all the time, Your lordship?' Mydar asked in astonishment.

'There is not much that escapes my attention, young warlock.'

'Uh… Do your best, Mydar…' The block on

Zendal's mind made it difficult for him to speak.

'You… can do it… Mydar,' Crasmont whimpered in the same state as his co-wizard. Mydar looked at Faal with contempt.

'If you harm them, I'll—' Mydar retorted.

Lord Faal burst into laughter. 'Don't worry, Mydar, they will not be harmed. It's just a type of mind freeze,' he said. 'They can't help you now. You're on your own, boy.' The Demonite Lord sniggered, returned to his place and closed his eyes – as did Mydar.

A small bead of sweat streamed down the warlock's forehead and dripped off his nose onto his sleeve. The only sound heard was the whistling wind, rustling through the woodland. All eyes were fixed on the small stone nestled in a snow cup. A long silence fell between the two opponents and the cold air hung like a weight around Mydar's shoulders.

A sudden shudder emitted from the stone and it began to drift towards Mydar's line. Crasmont's eyes almost bulged out of his head. Slowly, the stone floated closer and closer. The young warlock felt its presence and his stomach tightened. He breathed in deeply and filled his mind with the wizardry of a thousand years.

A broad smile filled the Demonite's face, but the stone hovered within a couple of inches of the line and stopped… More beads of sweat glazed Mydar's brow as his eyebrows trembled, and then calmness consumed the fear. It was as if his mind was filled with the strength of a thousand warlocks.

Lord Faal was still smiling until the rock shuddered and began to move in his direction. Suddenly the smile turned to a stony grimace. Mydar began to use the skill and experience he had been taught by Zendal over the years. The grey stone was forced along an invisible path towards the Demonite.

Zendal was filled with pride watching his former apprentice becoming a wizard worthy of the throne. One day, Zendal would relinquish his position and he now saw that Mydar would make a creditable successor.

Teetering on the brink of Faal's line, however, the stone slowed pace and reversed! Lord Faal pushed his mind to the limit and forced the object back at Mydar. Crasmont and Zendal both looked on open-mouthed and held their breath. Mydar dug deep inside himself and held on for all he was worth. The stone floated back to its original position in the centre and hovered about a foot or so above the ground. The rock was caught in a magic deadlock and held fast. Both sides were so focused and strong that, after a minute or so, the rock exploded into a fine dust and peppered the ground. Each opponent collapsed on their backs, exhausted and breathing deeply. The Demonite audience sighed in the background. The glowing rings were lifted away from Zendal and Crasmont and they grabbed the young wizard tightly.

'Well done, Mydar,' Zendal burst out with glee.

'I knew you could do it,' Crasmont added excitedly.

'But I didn't win,' he whimpered pathetically, feeling weak and feeble.

'No, but you didn't lose either,' Faal responded honestly.

'What does this mean?' Mydar asked as he sat up.

'It means it's a draw. I've never lost before and you didn't win this time,' Lord Faal answered cunningly, although he did sound disgruntled not to be victorious.

'Can we have out amulets back, then?' Crasmont asked.

'I am a Demonite of my word. You are free to go and you can have your amulets. It was a very noble fight, Mydar,' he said, walking over and patting the wizard's shoulder. 'Reed, these wizards are no longer an enemy of our people; they are free to go,' he announced and nodded.

'Bring the amulets,' Reed said with a smile and gently grabbed Mydar's arm in friendship.

A slightly shorter and younger Demonite steered through the crowd of people who were now standing and clapping their hands in appreciation. There was a pouch attached to his waist and he reached in and pulled out three blue necklaces. The wizards' joy at being reunited with their precious power stones soon turned to fear and concern. They glanced at each other and then back at the amulets, their hearts sinking.

'What's wrong?' Lord Faal asked, seeing the obvious dismay on their faces.

'The stones are losing power. The last time this happened was many years ago when Evilan had taken the kingdom,' Zendal confessed.

'What does this mean, Zendal?' Reed's face tightened slightly.

'It means things have proceeded much more quickly than I had anticipated,' Zendal answered with a heavy heart and turned to Lord Faal. 'Before we go, I have something I must say. It concerns your safety and the safety of everyone in and outside Wizards' Kingdom,' Zendal said seriously.

Lord Faal took him to one side and they talked for a while. Supplies of food and water were given to the travellers in friendship. After the short meeting, in which Zendal explained the grave situation that was hanging over them all, he and Lord Faal returned.

'Reed, we must prepare for battle. Our lives are under threat,' Lord Faal called out.

'What is happening, Your Lordship?' the Demonite asked urgently.

'I will explain later,' he answered and turned to Zendal.

'We must be on our way. When the time is right, I will send word to you, Lord Faal; I promise,' Zendal said with conviction and turned to depart.

★

The four travelers – Zendal, Shim, Crasmont and Mydar – made their way to the hills and waved to their new-found friends.

'It's happening all over again,' Crasmont said, biting his lower lip.

'Yeah, I know what you mean, Crasmont,' Mydar confirmed, his mind racing.

'We need all the help we can get this time,' Zendal said as they disappeared into the distance.

CATCHET'S KINGDOM

Treela felt cold and weak, his head hurt and his eyes were sore. He looked around and sucked in breath urgently. He was on his knees in the courtyard of Spellock Castle. He was surrounded by people who worked in and around the castle. There were also several keepers from the other castles in the kingdom who had come to help defend Spellock and the kingdom from the enemy. More troops were on their way, but what could they do now? Everyone looked so lost and frightened. Then realisation dawned on Treela and it all came flooding back to him like a bad dream. They had been turned to stone by an evil spell. Now, although they were prisoners, they had at least had the use of their limbs returned to them.

They were captured in their own castle by the ruthless army of Loof and Evilan. The bird creatures were perched along the tops of the walls, almost statue-like themselves. There were thousands there: on the towers, on the inner turrets, and on the tops of the balconies and steeples. On the ground, the other beasts were roaming everywhere – the 'pig-people', as Treela had once mockingly called them, but he would not dare to do so now.

Now everything was different. These monsters weren't myths talked about around campfires, stories of old; they were real, they were here and, worst of all, they were in charge.

Someone called Treela's name and he joined the prisoners as they were herded down into the very dungeons that had imprisoned Lord Torsk all those years ago. Pushed like sheep, the crowd moved along, grim-faced and terrified.

'Drentar,' Treela called out, but Drentar glared back and put a finger to his lips, signifying silence.

Treela looked back, open-mouthed, and then dropped his head in shame. *What a stupid thing to do*, he thought, *we must not let the outsiders know who the leaders are.*

Outside, the skies were still a dull, neutral grey and the ground was hard and frozen, like the hearts of their captors. Inside, the murky tunnels leading to the dungeons were black and cold and had not been used for many, many years. Groups of people were separated off at random into the various cells. One or two of the younger men retaliated against the over-bearing force used by the Seeker soldiers, only to be beaten back into place with grunts and squeals of impatience.

As luck would have it, especially as luck was in very short supply, Treela was placed with the group in Drentar's cell. They were forcibly shoved in through the metal doorway. The heavy clank of the door shutting behind them was enough to make the strongest heart quicken. Inside, there were about fifty prisoners crammed into the small space.

'You all right, boy?' Drentar murmured. His face was lined and his mind tormented with deep thoughts.

'Yes, sir, I'm fine,' Treela replied graciously.

There was a sudden commotion from behind and

the two turned in curiosity. The bulk of prisoners had gathered at the rear of the cell and seemed to be crowding round something. Drentar pushed forward, as did Treela.

'It's incredible,' one voice uttered.

'It can't be him,' said another.

'Come on now, let me through,' Drentar commanded as he bore his way through the tightly-knit bunch. Not to be left behind, Treela quickly followed on before the gap sealed itself. The last few people parted as Drentar and Treela stopped... Treela let out an inadvertent gasp.

A solid rock statue of Evilan rested at the back of the cell. For a short while no one said anything; everyone stood mesmerised.

'This means only one thing—' Drentar began.

'Loof is in command,' Treela cut in and then realised and looked at Drentar in apology.

'Why have we been brought back from statues?' someone chirped from the crowd.

'It would have been much easier for Loof if everyone was encased in stone – one less thing for him to worry about,' commented another.

'Just think about it,' Drentar explained, 'Loof has control of the whole kingdom, he has an unbeatable army and, to top it all off, he has Crockledam's amulet and the great Orb.' The mention of Crockledam silenced the room; they all knew the greatest force to defeat Loof and defend their castle was gone and they had no idea where the wizards were – if, indeed, they were still alive.

'Meaning?' came a puzzled voice from the crowd.

Drentar shook his head in disbelief. 'Meaning, what threat are we going to cause? Not much! We are imprisoned with no weapons and surrounded by Kites and Seekers by the thousands,' he said bitterly.

'So that's it then, it's over?' another voice croaked out from an old man at the back.

'No… I didn't say that. We have to get word to the wizards somehow, if they are still alive,' Drentar retorted.

Everyone stood silent for a while.

'It's the end; we are lost,' a gloomy voice again surged from the back.

'I could get word to the wizards,' a single voice chirped through the quiet.

All eyes steered towards the person who had uttered this and then mocking laughter rang out. Treela realised how his outburst sounded and stood red-faced and embarrassed.

'Silence!' Drentar erupted. 'Have any of you got a plan?' The laughter stopped.

The sudden noise from the cell caused a curious Seeker to investigate. The creature came to the iron gate and stared inside. For a short while it just stood, peering with eyes of anger and fire. Everyone turned and stared back in fear. It raised his right arm and, clutching its club, rattled the cage violently, grunting and squealing menacingly. Everyone in front shuffled back a few steps. Once the creature had had its fun, it sneered and turned away. A couple of prisoners tentatively approached the bars and watched as the dwarf Seeker eased out of sight.

'Give the boy a chance, let him speak,' Drentar

commanded. 'Have any of you got any kind of plan?' Drentar repeated in a whisper, his eyes filled with fire that cut through the prisoners like a knife. Inside, however, Drentar's confidence wavered. He hoped that his faith in the boy would prove justified. He looked at Treela and nodded in encouragement.

'I have a Calamander bird,' Treela said softly. Drentar frowned, then widened his eyes in anticipation of an explanation.

'It… It's a homing bird. It follows the path to its master,' Treela stammered unconvincingly.

'But Treela, if it's your bird it will find *you*,' a voice commented sarcastically.

'Ermm…' Drentar coughed and flashed a glance of disapproval.

'That's the point,' Treela blasted back. 'It's King Zendal's pet bird. He gave it to me a couple of years ago to look after for him. He visits it now and again.'

'Continue, Treela,' Drentar said with interest.

'I could release it and send it to our king with a message. But there is a problem – it's in a cage in the stables.' Treela finished what he had to say and lowered his head, remembering that they were underground in the dungeons and the stables were across the courtyard up above.

'That's one problem I may be able to help you with, Treela,' Drentar said, winking at the young lad. Drentar is Crasmont's apprentice and his master had taught him many things. Although he could never give him his amulet until his death, he did teach him many spells and mind tricks. 'We'll wait until things are quieter later and then we can set out a plan,' Drentar announced with relish. Gathering the prisoners around him, he told them what he was going to do.

As luck would have it, the army began to settle for the night – although no one could tell whether it was night or day in the permanent winter gloom. In the courtyard, on the walls, and outside in the surrounding fields, the army was scattered like pebbles on a beach. Only one guard patrolled the dungeons – with the prisoners locked away they were no threat. Drentar's mind cleared of all thought and he concentrated on the guard.

Another piece of luck for the captives was the fact that it was a Seeker that guarded them and not a Kite. Seekers have very little brainpower and their minds are easier to penetrate than the mind of a Kite. The apprentice wizard sat cross-legged on the ground with the tips of his index fingers pressed gently against each temple. He was nervous; he had only attempted the 'mind shift' once, and that was on Crasmont in an experiment a few years earlier. It had worked, but he was not totally convinced he could do it again. The pressure weighed like a boulder on his shoulders. The plan was to get the Seeker to open the cell door so that Treela could take the message they had written, attach it to the bird and let it fly to Zendal – if he was still alive. Drentar had explained there was no point in everyone trying to escape. There were so many soldiers, he told them, that they would all get caught before they had a chance to get away. He had explained earlier that evening that if the mind shift worked he could use it to better advantage for them all to escape at a later time.

He concentrated hard and rubbed gently on his temples. The Seeker wandered past the cells and, as it came to theirs, paused! Stillness prevailed for a short time as everyone waited, but it continued its patrol. The prisoners looked on in dismay. Drentar was still concentrating and suddenly jerked back his head. Inside the depths of his mind another voice came flooding through.

Drentar, concentrate, I will help you. Drentar didn't recognise the voice for a moment. Then suddenly it hit him: it was Candor, Mydar's apprentice.

With renewed vigour they pooled their energies and flooded the simple mind of the Seeker guard again. This time it stopped and turned slowly. Sluggishly, it ambled back to Drentar's cell and, in a trance-like state, reached for the key, slipped the tip into the rusty lock and clicked it open. Once the job was done it removed the key, slipped it back on the hook on its belt and returned to its routine. Drentar blinked open his eyes and stretched back his head. The smiles on the faces of the other prisoner told the story.

'Treela, take the message and free the bird,' Drentar said.

'Why him? I could do that,' the voice of the impatient prisoner, Zool, ranted.

'I've explained all this once, Zool. Treela knows where the bird is, he also knows the stables and castle like the back of his hand,' Drentar continued impatiently, 'which is good because, as it's dark, he can hide his small frame in the shadows.' Zool relented and nodded in agreement.

Treela's heart pounded with fear as he left the safety

of the cell. He felt weak and very tired as he realised the full importance of his mission. He carried the whole weight of Wizards' Kingdom on his puny shoulders. He set his mind on the job ahead and scuttled along the dark corridors. Light from burning torches glowed through the blackness of underground passages. He came to the end of the passageway.

The Seeker guard now lay grunting in its sleep at the base of the stairs. He knew he had to step over the creature to gain entrance to the staircase, so he quietly tiptoed towards the beast.

The Seeker's pig-like head rested on the bottom step and its right arm was strewn across the next two above. The boy quietly sucked in a lung-full of air and eased himself close to the beast's armpit. A disgusting animal aroma rose from the beast and it almost made the boy heave. Treela lifted his right leg and placed his foot on the step between the creature's head and shoulder. All went well as he balanced his body to lift off on his left foot. He steadied his pose and lifted his leg, but his toe flicked the hairs under the beast's armpit.

A huge grin appeared on the Seeker's face and it dropped its arm, closing the gap on Treela's left foot and clamping it to its side – his foot was now trapped! Panic took over and Treela's heart raced frantically; his shallow breathing became rapid and his mind was a whirl of confusion. The stench rising up his nostrils was almost too much to bear. He clenched his fists tightly and closed his eyes. *Think, Treela, think*, he told himself.

He stopped and wiped his mind of dread. He bent

down close to the monster's face and gently blew into its right ear. Up close and personal to the Seeker, concentration was the only way to stop the queasy feeling in Treela's stomach. The creature stirred and lifted its hand to scratch the menacing insect it thought was annoying it. With that small chance, as the hairy arm released his trapped leg, Treela fled quickly upwards, leaving the unsuspecting guard to its piggy dreams.

Speeding away, Treela waited a few seconds before daring to breathe in the damp stale air. It was much better than the stench of the Seeker.

Outside, the air was cold and crisp and Treela shivered. The blast of winter air on his face sharpened his wits to his task. Treela was more exposed here, but the soldiers were not paying much attention, so he easily made his way unseen to the stables. He flitted here and there, avoiding open areas, and came upon the barn door, which was luckily ajar. He slipped inside and walked gingerly along the unlit passageway. To either side the horses were leaning their heads out over the half doors of their compartments. They recognised the boy straightaway and weren't nervous when he stroked them one by one as he passed. At the bottom end of the stable, his object came into view. The bird cage hung on a big hook that was fixed to a wooden ceiling beam. The blue, green and yellow Calamander stood quietly on its perch.

Treela's body filled with hope and for the first time he felt confident... until he looked to either side, where the hay was kept. Treela dipped down, observing the two piles of hay with a Kite sleeping on each one. He gritted his teeth and almost called out in a curse. How on earth was he going to get the bird now?

He refocused on the job at hand and thought of the things that King Zendal had always taught him. *There is always a way around a problem*. The king's words came bursting back to him. Treela dropped on all fours and crawled along the floor. He was used to the smell and it wasn't as bad as the pig soldier. Without a sound, he positioned himself under the cage and slid up the wall. The cage had two little doors: one at the front and the other underneath. He reached to the underside of the cage.

The Kites fidgeted and rustled on their hay beds, chirping and screeching at a low pitch. Treela's fingers grasped the trapdoor and turned the latch, opening it. Bird droppings and sawdust came fluttering down on Treela's face and open mouth. He winced and used his left hand to scrape the mess off his tongue and face. He screwed up his face in disgust, but stayed totally silent.

Treela swiftly turned left and right and saw the two Kites were still napping peacefully. He reached into the cage and clamped the Calamander in his palm – moving quickly, like a lizard catching a fly. The little bird had no time to move or call out. Its body warmed Treela's palm.

He panted a sigh of relief, then felt something wriggle and pinch his leg. Curiously, he looked down. It was a big, black, beady-eyed rat. He tensed. He still had one hand free, with the other holding the bird. Slowly, the rodent made a path up his leg. Treela had seen loads of rats as he cleaned out the stable on a regular basis; that didn't make him like them, though! He breathed in deeply and, as the creature began to climb his stomach, he closed his eyes and reached out, then simply flicked it off with his hand. Annoyed, the rodent scuttled away to the corner and disappeared. Amazingly, the two bird soldiers were still dozing and didn't notice as Treela made his way back outside.

The young stable boy found a quiet spot and lovingly stroked the bird to ease its nervousness. First, he attached a small piece of leather with a message from Drentar to the Calamander's leg using a ball of twine from his pocket and tied it firmly. He then kissed the bird fondly on the head and whispered something in its ear. The bird fidgeted in his hand and he released it. With a flutter of wings and a new-born freedom, the Calamander soared high into the sky. Treela looked for a moment, wanting to escape and feel as free as that bird. Then his heart sank; he knew he had to make his way back down to the dungeon and not give the game away.

★

High up in the tower the small but powerful Catchet surveyed his new domain and strolled out onto the cold stone rampart. He rested his hands on the tower's battlements and looked out at his new kingdom. The fading light unveiled hordes of darkened figures splayed across the open fields of Spellock. *This is my kingdom*, he whispered to himself.

A small bird flew past the tower and caught his eye

as it fluttered away into the darkness. It occupied his attention only for a moment and then he turned and made his way back to his new life.

The Calamander soared brave and strong into the distant night with only one path in mind. Its wings beat hard and fast as it sped away into the chilled evening air.

THE SIGNAL

Zendal stood on the ridge of rocks that eased away from the cliffs and pointed, like a granite finger, to the stars. For the first time in what seemed like an age, he could actually see the stars glinting dimly behind the dirty grey shield. He dearly missed his homeland and his people; he even missed the tedious day-to-day tasks that kings must do.

A while earlier they had left the Demonite camp and travelled for some distance. They were no longer in woodland, but in a more rocky terrain. Crasmont and Mydar were snuggled around the glowing embers of their campfire.

Something had shaken Zendal from his slumber – a feeling, a deep fluttering in his very soul – so he had walked outside. The air held the chill of mid-winter, but he couldn't take his eyes from the broad spectrum of the universe. A sad, sad pain of despair had filled his heart and flooded his mind earlier that day. It was the same feeling that had consumed him when Veltzeg passed away, but what had caused it this time?

He knew something was very wrong in Wizards' Kingdom, but was too afraid to delve into his warlock's intuition to find the answer. Crasmont's snoring broke his concentration and he turned to check on his companions. There they lay, like two children: loyal, obedient and so close to his heart…

Something caught his attention; a flickering in the corner of his eye, from far off a fluttering of wings, drew closer and closer. The old wizard stared in anticipation. As the object neared, Zendal realised what it was. A spark of excitement lit up his glassy gaze. It was his Calamander bird – a present once given to him by the very person he later loathed... Lord Torsk!

The bird circled round his head and landed gently at his feet. Zendal stepped back a couple of paces, instinctively knowing what the Calamander bird was going to do next. Calamander birds normally carried messages – there was one tied to its leg – but Zendal knew that the bird was about to give him another message. The brightly-coloured bird stood still and spread its wings. Its tiny frame began to glow and expand. A shaft of light emitted from its body and released an image. The translucent red beam lifted to around four foot high. Zendal looked on in anticipation; he had seen this spectacle unfold once before. The shape of a tall, human form emerged through the blinding, bleached-white aura. It was the familiar, but surprising shape of Lord Torsk. This was the once-respected ruler of Wizards' Kingdom, killed by Zendal in battle many years ago. His eyes were black and clear, his stance stern and true.

'Crockledam…' The low tone of his voice cut through the whistling wind. 'Crockledam,' he continued, 'has fallen.' The steady flow of his voice faded. A lump came to Zendal's throat and a tear streamed from the corner of his eye. He restrained his remorse and held on to his dignity.

'You need help this time, Zendal. I can do nothing but warn you. The kingdom is sealed and Loof commands.' There was a slight pause before the old ruler continued. 'Evilan is also slain; he stands in the dungeon, locked in granite, never to be reborn. The people are all prisoners now too,' he concluded.

'Lord Torsk, why are you warning me now after everything that's happened in the past?' Zendal questioned with distrust.

'I was a fool in life. Now, in spirit, I have realised the evil I did to Veltzeg, and what I allowed Evilan to do. I should have stopped him long ago and maybe things would have been different.' He stared at his successor and then carried on. 'With regret, this message is all I can do to put things right. Zendal, you must kill Loof.'

'Loof was good once and he can be again,' Zendal retorted.

'It's too late, Zendal. I fear the evil has eroded his soul… It's too late.' Torsk's image then evaporated and was swallowed back into the Calamander's minute body. Nightfall reclaimed its place and Zendal stood alone again, filled with sadness and anger. *Is this the end?* he asked himself.

A lonely chirp brought him out of his reverie. The colourful creature peered at Zendal with its beady eyes, as if to say goodbye. With a tiny flutter of wings, the bird burst into flight. The Calamander soon disappeared into the curtain of black and Zendal turned towards his companions. Unaware of anything that had taken place, the two wizards were still sleeping soundly. Even Shim, the lightest of all sleepers, hadn't noticed the incident that had just taken place. Zendal decided not to wake them; he'd wait until morning to reveal the devastating news.

★

Morning eventually came, after what seemed like a long spell of waiting for the sleepless Zendal. The dawn was just as dim as it had been ever since Jarrak's death. Crasmont and Mydar eventually stirred and woke.

'What is it, Zendal?' Crasmont asked, immediately noticing the torment on the king's aged face. Mydar looked on in anguish as Zendal conveyed the message that the Calamander bird had brought.

'We've done it before and we can do it again, Zendal, even if it is Loof and not Evilan this time.'

Crasmont's body stiffened defiantly and he clenched his fist.

'He was our friend, but if he's become our enemy now I'll fight him to the death for Wizards' Kingdom,' Mydar ranted.

'I'm at a loss this time, friends. Our amulets are fading, so our magic is low; we had Loof to help us against Evilan, now though…' He trailed off, dropping his head forward and his chin to his chest.

'With respect, I'll have no talk like this, Master,' Mydar piped up. 'We will fight to the death to regain our land!'

A glow of pride filled Zendal's heart. He knew then that if they survived this last battle then Mydar would become a great leader. With fresh determination, the three wizards prepared for one last push, with Shim at their side. The outlook was bleak, but they set out on their onward journey with more resolve than ever before.

They travelled twenty miles or so over snow-covered, rocky country. The area seemed familiar, but with the winter scene it was difficult to say. Something caught the young wizard's eye and he let out a gasp. He rubbed both his eyes and squinted into the distance.

'Is that…?' He stopped and stood mesmerised with excitement.

'My goodness!' Crasmont exclaimed. Zendal was already looking on in disbelief. A lone structure stood amidst the vast sea of white-crusted landscape. The wizards recognised the well straightaway. They moved a little closer and Shim gave out a loud snort.

'We've come full circle, my friends. That's got to be

the entrance to Veltzeg's castle,' Zendal declared confidently.

'And it has tunnels leading to Spellock castle,' Crasmont recalled, filled with renewed excitement.

'This could be the break we need,' Mydar interjected with a broad smile on his face. It was as if they had been handed a fantastic favour from somewhere.

'Yes but, if you remember, Loof's spell sealed it off with an iron door,' Zendal prompted.

'Well, we'll have to break the spell. It's our only way in, without giving ourselves away,' the chubby wizard said with a steely glare.

'That's if Loof hasn't set a trap. He might remember, you know,' Zendal chipped in.

'Yes, but if he had remembered the tunnel, he wouldn't have put the prisoners down there. He would have set his troops down there in readiness,' Mydar added sensibly, making Zendal and Crasmont stare at each other in surprise.

Without any further talk, Mydar moved in, climbed over the top and disappeared down into the murky depths. Just behind him, Crasmont followed. As Zendal entered, he suddenly called a halt to the proceedings. Everyone reluctantly returned to the top.

'What is it, Zendal? We're wasting valuable time,' Crasmont muttered as Mydar's head broke the surface.

'What about Shim?' Zendal's companions looked at one another and then back at the stallion. Zendal peered into Shim's eyes and brushed his hand down Shim's long snout. 'I'm going to have to leave you for a while, boy,' the old wizard relayed with sadness. Shim just stared back blankly.

They left some food for the animal and, stroking Shim's broad back one last time, Zendal turned and all three sorcerers disappeared down into the blackness.

From the bottom of the well, the wizards looked up into the dim light and saw Shim's head peering over the rim.

'It'll be all right, boy. We'll come back soon, I promise,' Zendal called sadly.

Ahead of them was a long, sinister-looking tunnel. It had been many years since they had travelled this way and Zendal remembered the last time he had journeyed there.

'There was an amber light the last time we entered,' Mydar remembered.

'Ah yes, I remember now – the orangey-yellow ball King Veltzeg held as his power.' Crasmont's mind was ablaze with old memories.

'He combined it with Loof's power, creating the super energy surge we used to enter the castle all those years ago,' Zendal reminisced.

'What happened to the ball? There's no light down here now,' Crasmont noted.

'It must have died with him,' came Zendal's answer.

With no light to guide them, the three blind warlocks held onto one another's robes as Zendal took the lead. The amulets were far too dim to throw any light.

They followed the trail deep underground. Above them, the icy blanket of winter covered the Cascoo desert. After what seemed like miles of walking, they came in contact with a cold, flat wall and it sparked another familiar memory.

'This must be the metal door that led into Veltzeg's Kingdom; it's just got to be,' the old wizard said with conviction.

It hadn't been opened for a long time and so the three wizards heaved against it. It cracked at first and gave way slightly. With extra pressure it eventually snapped open and creaked to its full width. Beneath them, the floor felt as smooth as when they had first entered the building, so many years before.

Mydar felt along the nearest wall and grasped a stake that had been long extinguished. There was still some dry gauze attached to the end. He then tried something he'd never done before, but had seen Zendal do many times. He pointed his index finger at the tip of the stick and concentrated. The others were unaware what was happening as they too were groping round, looking for some kind of light. His mind went into a wizard state and his index finger began to glow, gradually at first, and then strongly with a scarlet shade of red. The colour reflected in Mydar's face. When Crasmont looked at what Mydar was doing, his heart skipped a beat.

Zendal knew at once what was happening and watched as a burst of magical energy projected from Mydar's finger and caressed the timber. The reddish tongue licked the wood and gauze until it sparked into a live flame.

'Well done, Mydar, excellent!' Zendal beamed.

'We'll make a wizard of you yet,' Crasmont re-marked sarcastically with a wink.

Mydar, amazed at his new powers, smiled at his

own achievement. With the torch now flaming away brightly, they found more torches and lit them. The room was alive again and the memories came flooding back: the stone-clad floor, the huge wooden table, the wall-to-wall collection of books, and the drapes and other fixtures that were the heart and soul of King Veltzeg's castle.

Inside, the temperature was strangely warmer than that of the freezing tunnel. There, on the vast table, the most beautiful leather-bound book lay, untouched for years. This book, Zendal remembered, was the very book Veltzeg had used to change into Shim and back again. Would it be possible to change Shim into something that could come down the well and join them?

Zendal walked over to the book, dusted off the thick film of age, and gently lifted it open.

'What are you doing, Master?' Mydar quizzed.

'I think I know. It's Shim, isn't it?' Crasmont asked.

With a nod of his head, Zendal flipped over page after page until he came upon the Changing Spell. Using his many years of wizarding skills and experience, he chanted the words from the spell. Nothing happened for a minute or so, but then… a cool gust of air swirled round the room. *Whoosh!*

A form appeared in the middle of the room. All three pairs of eyes locked onto the strange apparition. A sketchy outline came at first; eventually a small, brownish figure, about four feet tall, stood up.

'My word!' was all Crasmont could spill from his mouth.

'Good grief!' Mydar gasped and Zendal smiled with

surprise at what he had conjured up.

Slowly, the figure forged itself into a solid state and stood upright. There were now four figures in the room: Zendal, Crasmont, Mydar and Loof!

'What were you thinking, Zendal? Are you mad?' Crasmont exclaimed disrespectfully. Then, realising what he had said, offered sheepishly, 'Er... um, sorry.'

'That's all right, old man,' Zendal said, laughing. Mydar could say nothing, for once.

'Don't you see? We can infiltrate the castle with this Loof and no one will take any notice until it's too late,' Zendal said with total conviction.

'It's a bit unnerving though, don't you think?' Crasmont asked.

'What is?' Zendal answered sarcastically.

'Travelling with Loof,' Mydar explained.

'Well, we know it's not him, don't we? So let's get our kingdom back,' he said and made his way to the secret wall panel that would lead to Spellock.

Zendal touched the uneven surface and, sure enough, it opened, uncovering the same pitch-darkness they had encountered in the outer passage. A chilled blast of air cut through the warmth of the throne room.

'Mydar, grab some torches. One each.' Zendal pointed to the wall. Crasmont took a flaming light from Mydar and waited.

'After you, er Shim... um... Loof, er,' Crasmont mumbled incoherently.

'Just treat him as you would normally treat Shim; he'll follow us as usual,' Zendal remarked and Mydar just shook his head. They moved steadily along the blackened tunnel.

'Are you all right, Shim?' Crasmont asked.

'Well he's not going to answer you is he, Crasmont? He's a horse!' Mydar sniped in a mocking tone. Zendal turned back and called his companion.

'Come here, Shim. Walk with me, boy. There, do you feel any easier now, Crasmont?'

'Sorry, Zendal, it just doesn't feel right somehow,' the chubby wizard said as he moved to one side for Loof to pass.

'We have a long trek ahead of us, so why don't we stay silent and conserve our energy,' Zendal said, grooming his beard with his free hand.

They travelled on for quite a while and all felt tired.

'It must be night-time, so let's get some rest and finish this journey in the morning,' the king announced.

They doused two of the three fire sticks and made camp for the night. They sat and ate what food and drink they had left and discussed their plans for once they reached Spellock Castle. Shim sat next to them and stayed silent. Crasmont and Mydar glanced uneasily at the little fellow every now and then, but eventually everyone slid into slumber.

They woke the next day from troubled sleep, wrestling with thoughts of their next encounter. The torch had burned down to a dull blue dome, so they quickly reignited the other two stakes before the torch finally died.

'Come on now, let's get a move on,' Zendal badgered.

'Are you feeling all right, Shim?' Crasmont asked, somehow expecting a reply.

'Crasmont, just because he looks like Loof doesn't mean he's going to talk. He never talked before he became Loof, so why should he talk now, you fool?' Zendal glared at him with impatience.

'Morning, Crasmont.' Mydar's voice echoed out of the darkness from behind Loof. It sounded just as if the little creature was talking. Crasmont looked at him in shock. Mydar then stepped forward, laughing at his joke and at the look on Crasmont's face.

'All right, all right you two, that's enough,' Zendal said seriously. 'We've a very important appointment ahead.'

Mydar took one of the torches, handed to him by Zendal, and took his normal position at the rear of the group. Shim walked silently by his master's side and Crasmont trailed behind them.

The journey took most of the day, but in the gloom of the deep tunnel no one could tell whether it was afternoon or evening. Zendal finally came to a halt.

'What is it, Master?' Mydar chirped from a little further back.

'I don't know, but I somehow recognise this part of the tunnel.' Zendal held up his flame and studied the ceiling. Crasmont trundled up beside him and craned his neck. The thick black veil of darkness moved away as Zendal guided the light forward. The four of them walked further along the path, keeping their eyes trained on the granite roof.

'Aha!' Zendal exploded. 'There it is!' The wizards strained to see what the dancing flame was showing.

'I don't believe it... It can't be.' The surprise in

Zendal's voice mystified both warlocks. He looked back at them.

'Don't you see?' he said urgently, pointing up towards the rocky ceiling.

About five feet above their heads was a trapdoor.

'You've found it, Zendal. Fantastic!' Crasmont expressed excitedly. Zendal looked at Crasmont and Mydar with disappointment. He blinked, rubbed his beard and explained.

'We should not have got this far.' He paused for a moment. 'The metal wall Loof created with his spell should have prevented us.' Many years earlier, when Loof and the wizards had gained entry to Spellock Castle from below, they had escaped through the same tunnel with Evilan's army in pursuit. At that time, Loof was working with the wizards to stop the Seekers and Kites from taking them prisoner. He had conjured a spell, creating a metal wall between them and the attacking army and giving the wizards a means of escape.

'Then what's happened? The spell must have dissolved when Loof's power changed,' Mydar insisted.

'It must have done,' Zendal said with a spark of real emotion. 'He probably doesn't even remember this place.'

'For once we might have a real advantage,' Crasmont added with a smile.

'Right, let's waste no more time. We must get inside and prepare ourselves for a surprise attack,' Zendal urged.

'But there are only three of us, Zendal. Even with our people we are no match for Loof and his army,' Mydar said in a defeated tone.

'Mydar, there were only three of us when we fought at the shore of Shallow Water.' All of a sudden Loof stamped his foot with disapproval. 'Ah, I'm sorry Shim… four of us,' Zendal said sheepishly. 'Now come on, we're wasting time.'

The wizards gathered around the trapdoor, ready to start the next stage of their plan.

$\mathcal{F}$IRST $\mathcal{W}$AVE

$\mathcal{L}$oof sat on his throne, deep in thought. What was his next move going to be? His kingdom was sealed. *No one can defeat me!* The thought whirled through his head, but still a tiny doubt, a small glow of memory, tickled the back of his mind until he dismissed it.

★

Gently the bird glided and soared over the huge trees of Fettle Forest. It tipped its wings and swooped down between the twisted weave of branches and leaves. Down and down it coasted, darting here and there over wooden obstacles and under deformed knotted boughs. The roof of the forest kept out the harsh winter and sheltered the ground from heavy snowfall. The little Calamander settled on the windowsill of Plate's cottage and Flec called his father to look at the beautiful colours of its feathers. The bird displayed its grave message and, as quickly as it had come, it fluttered off to its next destination.

★

Mydar balanced on Crasmont's shoulders and reached up as high as he could. Zendal held the torch, shedding an imperfect source of light on the uneven, porous surface. Mydar stretched his fingers along the cold, sharp stone and came across the metal hatch. Once both hands were gripped tightly around the circular handle, he wrenched with all his might. He twisted and heaved and almost tipped himself and Crasmont over, but the door was stuck!

'Come on, Mydar… You're no light weight, you know,' Crasmont grunted under the ever-increasing pressure of his companion.

'Go on, Mydar, one last effort,' Zendal said with encouragement.

Mydar tensed himself; droplets of perspiration formed a line on his forehead. The wave of sweat seeped into his eyes like acid and gave him a burst of pain and energy. He pulled angrily at the handle and, to his surprise, felt the doorway loosen.

'That's it, Mydar, you've got it at last,' Zendal exclaimed excitedly.

'Come on, Mydar, I can't hold you much longer,' the short wizard bleated.

Mydar pulled one last time and the heavy metal door fell open. A pair of beady eyes peered at them through the gloom. Zendal raised his torch to identify the stranger.

'Treela!' Mydar burst out with astonishment, but the boy narrowed his eyes and touched his finger to his lips. Soon many more eyes appeared through the hole until a plethora of heads was in view. One by one, the wizards were pulled up into the murky dungeon.

A horrified voice cut through the shuffling and grappling. 'What is the meaning of this?'

Zendal turned to look, realised what had happened and smiled. 'Have no fear, he is not what he appears,' Zendal said. 'That is not Loof but Shim, my stallion. It was the only way I could get him through the tunnel.'

'A thousand pardons, Your Majesty,' the prisoner replied and pulled the little fellow up.

Everyone was now inside the cell and Zendal could see the fear and bewilderment in the prisoner's faces.

'Welcome, Your Majesty.' Drentar stepped forward. 'Candor is in an adjacent cell,' he told Mydar.

'What shall we do, O King?' Drentar asked.

'Begging your pardon, Your Majesty, but why don't we escape back through the tunnel?' Treela said nervously and all eyes peered at Zendal.

'Treela!' Drentar cut in swiftly.

'That's all right, Drentar. If anyone—' Zendal stopped short and everyone froze. The heavy thud of a Seeker's footsteps boomed through the passageways. Everyone turned and closed ranks, concealing the four new prisoners. The jailor shuffled along and came to a stop outside their cell. The creature reached to its side, grasping the large ring that held the key to each cell and unhooking it from his belt. It fumbled for a second or two and tried it in the lock. It turned it and it clunked – every prisoner's heart flipped at the sound. The door cracked open!

A snarl erupted from the Seeker's gaping mouth as the creature threw open the rusty door. Everyone directly in its path simultaneously sucked in breath and instinctively stepped back. The grotesque beast reached out and grabbed at anyone who got in its way, tossing them aside. Halfway inside the cell it stopped and leered at the frightened crowd. A sneer of contentment spread across its face. A lingering rasp of sound spilled from its mouth, almost certainly the equivalent of a laugh. Satisfied with the fear it had instilled, the pig creature turned to leave. It moved forward, but something stopped it from going any further. A flicker of suspicion flashed across its face and it pivoted back awkwardly. There, standing for all to see, was Zendal, his arm raised and his index finger pointing directly at the Seeker's chest. Without giving the Seeker time to squeal a warning call, a bolt of lightning fired from the tip of Zendal's finger and blasted a huge hole in the creature's armour. There was a whoosh of air, a cloud of brown powder and the creature was no more. Mumbled whispers filtered through the crowd as Zendal lowered his arm.

'This is it! We have no time to lose. The others will know soon enough when their companion doesn't report in,' Zendal said with conviction and sprung into action. 'Mydar, as quickly and as quietly as you can, open every cell door – but tell them all to be very quiet,' Zendal emphasised. 'Crasmont?'

'Yes, Master,' Crasmont answered immediately.

'Move all the elders and the children to the trap-door,' Zendal said.

'Yes, Master,' Crasmont repeated.

'Drentar, Candor, rig up a rope for everyone to climb down into the tunnel,' Zendal said pointing to the two apprentice wizards. 'We must get everyone who is incapable of fighting out of the castle and to safety.'

Everything the king asked for was done and gradually the weak were moved to safety down the tunnel.

'Now for our trump card,' Zendal said with relish, turning to Shim.

'Your Majesty, what is our plan?' Drentar asked politely.

'We must make our way to the throne room as quickly as possible with our decoy Loof ahead of us as if we've been captured.' Zendal went on, 'The Kites and Seekers won't suspect anything until it's too late.'

'What then, Your Majesty?' Candor enquired softly.

'Then comes the difficult part. We must enter the throne room and somehow overpower the real Loof and regain control of everything,' Zendal said, biting his lip in an unconvincing fashion. 'Remember, people, we've done it before, we can do it again. This is our kingdom,' he concluded with renewed vigour.

The people gathered in the passageways outside the cells with the wizards at the front. Zendal led the way with 'Loof' at his side and the rest followed. From the darkest depths of the dungeon they walked upwards through the castle, ever vigilant. They proceeded up the stairwell and into the main passageway. They passed through a room that a group of Kites and Seekers were using to sleep in when not on guard duty. Bodies were strewn on the floor and on windowsills in a comatose state, unaware of their impending doom. The three wizards bore down on them. In their wake, the people of Wizards' Kingdom, now a determined army, killed and disarmed the sleeping enemy as they passed through. By the time Zendal's company reached the door to the main hall, his people were well armed and every enemy encountered had been silently and efficiently killed.

'There's a guard!' Mydar whispered urgently through gritted teeth.

'I know, Mydar, stay calm,' Zendal replied with restraint and a calmness that only he could generate.

Crasmont's stomach churned as they got closer. The Seeker leaned towards them aggressively. 'Loof' ambled on in front of the others. He and the guard stared at each other and the guard shrank back in fear. The Seeker immediately turned and pushed open the door. The trickery was beginning to work and 'Loof' filed through (nudged by Zendal) and, tentatively, the wizards followed. As they walked past, the guards scrutinised each of the prisoners as if they were suspects in a crime.

In the corridor, the fake Loof walked on confidently. However, outside the dungeon he didn't know which way to go and stopped. Zendal took charge and moved alongside him. 'Loof' fell slightly behind his master.

The huge lobby led off to rooms in all directions and was meshed with a network of stairwells. The whole place was filled with the sleeping bodies of the enemy. *This is not going to be easy,* Zendal thought.

By now Zendal's own small army was emerging into the lobby, leaving piles of brown dust in its wake.

'We wait here until we get the signal,' Drentar whispered to Candor, pulling at his spear which had embedded itself in the door. Candor sent the message along the line of his now fully-armed troops.

Zendal and his team gently tiptoed through the mass of mangled bodies and eventually, without waking a single one, made their way to the passageway that led to the throne room.

This is going far too well, Crasmont thought

suspiciously. There were no guards at this point and the wizards couldn't believe their luck. As quietly as they could, the three pushed open the large oak door and continued inside.

'There hasn't been much in the way of retaliation, Master. It's as if the enemy are immune to attack; as if they know they can't be defeated,' Mydar said.

'This could be a trap or maybe Loof really isn't expecting an attack from this angle,' Zendal whispered.

The narrow passage leading to the throne room didn't have any Kites or Seekers strewn over the floor. This area was kept clear for the new king's privacy. There was, however, one guard – a Kite hanging upside down like a bat over the doorway. This Kite was supposedly guarding Loof's door, but was in an obvious state of deep sleep.

The wizards approached with caution. Zendal signalled to the others to stay put and, with 'Loof' by his side, came within touching distance of the Kite.

Kites look menacing the right way up, but at this angle the creature was even less appealing. Unfazed by its dormant state, Zendal gestured to the wizards to move past. Suddenly, the creature's yellowy eyes flickered open. In a flash it was standing on the ground and eyeing up the intruders with distaste. The vile beast was just about to strike the wizard down when it reeled back in utter surprise at the sight of 'Loof'. Confused, the Kite looked at the Catchet and watched his movements as he trundled past him. Still not quite sure what was going on, the guard weighed up the situation and darted a suspicious glare back at Zendal; but before it could retaliate it exploded into fine dust. Zendal stood with his arm outstretched, his fist still closed around the air where the creature's throat had been a moment before.

'Well done, Master,' Mydar blurted out.

'Shh,' Zendal whispered angrily.

One last door was the only obstacle left between them and the unsuspecting Catchet. Once opened, they quietly inched inside the almost lightless den. Each creak seemed to cut through the darkness and a real fear gripped even Zendal. Everyone split up to cover more ground in less time. The throne stood empty and left Zendal with a cold feeling. Next to it the Orb, still placed on its pedestal, was deathly cold and still.

'Master, where is he?' Mydar called out.

'Keep quiet, you fool,' Zendal burst back bitterly.

'Master he's—' Crasmont gasped and was lifted off the ground, his body rotating clockwise at great speed. The Orb's stagnant colour began to whirl into life, turning the inky black colour of evil. Loof was nowhere to be seen.

Crasmont's body dropped to the floor and hordes of Kites started pouring through the room's windows. At the same moment, Shim's body changed back into its stallion form. A loud crashing sound came from behind as countless Seekers invaded the scene. The whole room ignited into a full-blown battle.

Crasmont regained composure and joined his fellow warlocks. The wizards immediately tried to draw on the power of the Orb, but Loof still held control of it. They had to improvise and drew magical strength from one another. Their minds melded as one and they all sucked power from within. Countless centuries of wizardry, spells and magic were brought forth in a colossal groundswell that overwhelmed even the mighty Orb.

Zendal, Crasmont and Mydar's bodies levitated and a mystical inner light shone through them. It illuminated their eyes and gave mammoth energy to their fingertips. By now the room was filled with grunting, screaming and shrieking enemy soldiers. Kites leapt at the wizards only to explode instantly into fine powder. Seekers surrounded the shining warriors and attacked in force, only to expire in the same manner as their bird-like companions. From the corridor came Zendal's own people, armed to the teeth with the weapons taken from the sleeping army. They swarmed across the battleground. The wizards moved in a line through one of the windows and hurtled outside into the advancing dawn.

Waiting in the fields and the surrounding castle grounds, hundreds of thousands of Loof's army were in full battle mode. Ninety percent of his Kites were already airborne and all of his foot soldiers were surging forward. The true battle was about to begin.

'Crasmont, you are a good friend and a loyal wizard,' Zendal conveyed with deep conviction. 'Mydar, you too are everything I hoped you'd be. Whatever happens, may Wizards' Kingdom prevail!' he concluded and all three wizards broke away and dived into full battle.

Mydar landed on one of Spellock's towers and was immediately engaged with hundreds of Kites. He raised his hands and splayed his fingers. A tangled network of white energy erupted from the tips of his fingers and obliterated the first wave of intruders, sending clouds of dirty brown dust to pepper the virgin-white snow; but then came another wave and another.

Crasmont touched down in the courtyard and stood in the centre, surrounded by thousands of grunting Seekers and squealing Kites. Like a child's spinning top, the tubby wizard began to spin faster and faster. Blinding sparks of ultraviolet light whipped and crackled from his body. At full speed, he changed into a whirling wizard tornado. The soldiers approached in droves only to be tossed to the four winds.

Zendal glided across the dirty, matted sky and locked in battle with swarms of deadly Kite soldiers. He dipped and lifted in flight, aiming waves of missiles that slammed into their targets, smashing them to smithereens.

The foot soldiers regrouped and stopped pushing forwards. Instead, they stood their ground and, with their spears aimed at the spinning hurricane of Crasmont, began to throw their weapons. This was unexpected. The Seekers were usually incapable of independent logic. Suddenly, they were using their brains and thinking about the best way to fight. This use of brainpower interfered with the wizards' magic and weakened Crasmont's energy.

Mydar's lightning show destroyed thousands of the enemy, but behind them more came and behind them even more. Zendal darted through the stagnant clouds, thumping great holes in the Kite barrier, but the skies were still full of the screeching creatures. Inside the throne room the apprentice wizards and Zendal's army had, with few losses, taken out most of the enemy soldiers that had burst in on them. Shim was trampling the last of the Seekers and grinding them to dust. Their attention was now taken up by the war outside. Drentar and Candor looked through the open window to witness the vicious battle that was taking place around Spellock Castle. The three warlocks stood out like a brightly-lit fire in the depths of darkness, surrounded by a cloak of evil.

'What can we do to help, Drentar?' Candor asked meekly.

'There's not a lot we can do now, it's up to them. We don't have enough power to help,' Drentar solemnly replied. But after speaking these words, things began to change.

Crasmont's whirlwind began to slow and came to a shuddering stop. Mydar's lightning strikes started to weaken. Zendal also lost power and started falling from the sky. The three wizards locked forces like magnets and once more stood on the battleground together. They had fought well, but there were around ten thousand soldiers left out of the hundreds of thousands there had been to begin with. A lull swept across the battlefield. The remaining Seekers closed ranks again and were joined by their Kite comrades. The deafening screams of war died down until only the muttering of bird-beasts and Seekers could be heard.

'You have fought well, my friends, but we are weak and they are still strong,' Zendal admitted. A lump came to Crasmont's throat.

'Master, I will protect you to the end,' Mydar said defiantly.

'Master, so will I,' Crasmont bleated with tears in his eyes.

'Where is your master? Where is the mighty Loof?' Zendal shouted with eyes blazing at the deadly army, but there was no answer.

'Loof, come out and face us, you coward. Don't hide behind your pathetic army,' Zendal mocked. Still nothing moved, just a slight wind whistled overhead.

A sudden movement in the crowd caught Zendal's eye. A shuffling and a parting of soldiers revealed the King of Spellock Castle. The small, balding figure emerged from behind the tree-like legs of the Seekers. His round, beady eyes weren't sparkling like they used to – full of life and mystery. They were dull and blank and sapped of all joy. This was not the happy, helpful Loof of the past that the wizards loved. This Loof was emotionless and evil. This Loof wasn't really Loof at all, but a reincarnation of Jarrak. The Catchet was a shell of his former self and had been taken over completely by another. He opened his mouth to speak, but the voice that came out wasn't Loof's either, but that of Jarrak.

'Coward, you say? No, I'm no coward.' Jarrak's voice boomed out of Loof's tiny frame. 'Would a coward strike down the mighty Zendal?'

'Only a coward would use a huge army to conquer the might of three weak wizards,' Zendal mocked.

'Mmm, very clever Zendal, but not clever enough,' the Catchet snapped back at him.

'I know the real strength of the wizards of Wizards' Kingdom. Without the Orb you are nothing,' he rasped. 'And now my army has worn you down, I can finish you off. Not cowardice, but cleverness,' he said with a sickly tone, putting his fists on his hips and leering deep into Zendal's eyes.

'Now, you die…'

MARCH OF THE TROLLS

'I have at least ten thousand soldiers at my disposal and I haven't even used my own power yet.' The little Catchet giggled and continued, 'You've used up all your wizardly power leaving me the easy task of finishing you off.' His face glowed with satisfaction.

A twinge deep inside Zendal's heart made him pause for a moment, to ponder, before responding.

'You are right, Loof. Or Jarrak, or whoever you are,' Zendal replied.

'Master, you can't mean that!' Mydar said, gripping his master's shoulder. 'After all we've been through, you can't give up now.'

'Mydar's right, Zendal, we've never given up before; we've always fought to the end,' Crasmont said with a forlorn expression.

'It's over. Can't you see that, Crasmont? We've lost.' Zendal hung his head in defeat. Loof looked on in astonishment. This was even easier than he had thought it would be. He suddenly had a change of heart.

'I am not going to kill you after all. You will be my servants from now on,' Loof proclaimed.

'You can't let him get away with this, Master. Have you no dignity left?' Mydar exclaimed, shocked at his master's cowardice.

'Mydar, remember your place. You must still respect our king,' Crasmont reprimanded sharply, but he too felt that Zendal had let them down.

'I am king of this kingdom and no one else,' Loof exclaimed defiantly.

'But... Crasmont, don't you see what's happening here?' Mydar said. 'We can't let this evil, vile creature take over our kingdom.'

'I already have, or are you so dim-witted you can't even see that, you pathetic excuse for a wizard?' the Catchet said, throwing out his chest with pride.

★

A colossal surge of energy began to build below the ground. Tremendous temperatures expanded the gases trapped underground, forcing hissing steam up through the soil. The energy pulsed and throbbed in the network of tunnels that twisted their way underground. Scorching, toxic magma rolled and flowed in a smooth and deadly path, almost alive in its desire, surging up through Baldore Mountain.

First, vapour escaped up through the earth and out into open space. The scalding steam eased into the atmosphere, filtering through the sky, devouring and banishing the clouds. This was followed by grey volcanic dust, spewing clouds a hundred feet high. Suddenly the whole of Wizards' Kingdom rumbled, gently at first and then with increasing vigour. The vibrations became more and more violent.

A choking funnel of fumes forced its way out of the

mouth of Baldore Mountain and behind the fumes came its deadly secret. Lava gushed over the rim and poured out like a molten amber and charcoal waterfall. The thick, dirty-yellow liquid oozed down the mountain slope, melting and steaming its way through the snow-capped crest that had been Baldore's shroud for a thousand years. Now the volcano's cry was heard as it bellowed in anger from its very heart. Rivers of fire burst down into the valleys, suffocating and consuming everything in sight.

★

Spellock Castle trembled in fear of the distant volcano.

'What's happening?' The dishevelled voice of Loof was almost lost in the deafening roar of the eruption. Small chunks of masonry began cracking off the ancient castle and fell among the soldiers, causing death and injury. Kites and Seekers scattered in disarray.

'Zendal, what is going on?' Mydar called out.

'I don't know... I really don't!' he answered honestly.

'Soldiers, kill them! Kill them!' Loof shouted angrily, but as he spoke something else began to happen.

Stone missiles whistled through the air from a distance, smashing and exploding the soldiers. Loof turned around, steadying himself from falling as the ground continued to shake. More missiles rained down from the sky, sending Kites and Seekers into oblivion. The three wizards took their chance and slipped out of sight before Loof noticed.

From the horizon came an echoing war cry that rolled like a wave on the sea. Screams of pain and whimpers of defeat came from the ranks of Seekers. Thousands of Kites struggled to regain their composure and flew into the air to engage whatever was attacking them. The sky filled with the evil swarm of bird creatures, rising above the Seeker foot soldiers. Loof turned back to face the wizards, but they had gone!

'Attack, you fools, attack!' he shouted angrily, levitating high up into the sky with his Kite companions. The sight that met him was a total surprise. On the far outer edges of the lands surrounding Spellock Castle, a dark band had appeared across the white snow.

This new onslaught was from another source completely and Loof looked on in disbelief. This was another army, but its soldiers consisted of very different breeds. There were the Rock People of the Shallow Water in the front of the action. They were throwing the large boulders that were tearing through his ranks of Seekers. Behind them, ready to engage in battle, was a large group of Imps, gathered by Plate and Flec after they received the Calamander's urgent message. The normally peaceful forest people were armed with bows and were firing waves of arrows at Loof's army. Mixed in with the Imps and Rock People were the rest of the people of Wizards' Kingdom who had been hiding in the mountains and forests. Using whatever they could carry as weapons, they bravely joined the lines of this new army.

From the right flank came more help in the shape of Demonite soldiers, ready with their glowing bands of power. Deep in the background Loof could see, from his vantage point, the spewing angry mountain of Baldore. The volcano was puffing out clouds of grey smoke and oozing luminous golden sap from its tip. The ground continued to shudder under the tremendous pressure.

'Kill, kill, kill!' Loof ranted at his army in their native tongue. The bird-beasts swooped down to the front line and, with their claws flexed for action, swiped and slashed the Rock People. The stone-throwers were silent and quick. Before the birds had time to ravage the Rock People in front, they ducked down and the ones behind pelted the Kites with rocks. Screams of pain rang through the ranks as crowds of Kites exploded into clouds of dust. It didn't deter the angry beasts though and more attacked straight after, but the same fate awaited them.

There were still thousands of Seekers inside the castle walls and outside there was a greater number.

'Push forward, you snivelling fools,' Loof urged his troops on the ground and they started to surge.

Filtering through the crowd and lining up in front of the Rock People, the Demonites entered the battle. In spectacular fashion, the strangely tall, pale creatures linked their power bands and formed a barrier of orangey-red light. The translucent glow throbbed with a steady pulse and all the Demonites stood fast. After a couple of minutes the Seekers ambled on in attack, but as soon as their cumbersome frames touched the powerful beam they burst into nothingness.

The enemy's relentless onslaught continued for some time. The mighty Kites were smashing into this new army from above and the Seekers were trying to breach their lines from the ground. But with barrage after barrage of arrows and rocks stopping the birds from getting any closer, and the red band of hope now pushing the enemy back, things were changing. Loof's plan wasn't working. Floating up on high, he could see the front lines of his evil army slowly dwindling. Firmly, he ordered his subjects to retreat. His soldiers moved back into the castle and Loof shut the gates. The united army of people, Imps, Rock People and Demonites then surrounded Spellock Castle so no one could escape.

★

Meanwhile, the three good-hearted wizards had made their way back into the throne room. It was empty.

'Where have Shim and all the people gone, I wonder?' Zendal said.

'They must have joined the battle, Master,' Mydar surmised.

'Never mind that, we have more pressing things to do,' Crasmont said in an urgent manner.

The three wizards then located the Orb and tried to regain its powers.

'There's got to be a way of turning this whole mess around,' Mydar said positively. They started looking for spells that might do it.

★

Loof felt strange inside and knew something was happening with his Orb. He couldn't do anything at that time because he had to defend the castle from the new army. Outside the gates the Imps were poised to let loose a barrage of arrows over the walls and the Rock People were ready with an arsenal of rock missiles. The soldiers inside Spellock hushed, leaving only the wrath of the volcano's rumblings in the background.

Suddenly all heads lifted as two Kites came into view. The vile bird creatures flew overhead and displayed their trophy. Looking terrified and kicking and screaming Treela hung like a side of meat in a butcher's shop. Huge grins appeared on the Kite's grisly faces. In the next instant the gates parted, revealing a small group of prisoners including Shim, Drentar and Candor.

'So that's where they ended up, poor souls,' Zendal said as he looked on in dismay from the window.

In all this time a steady stream of lava was engulfing the land and the tremors were steadily getting stronger. Loof ordered that the gates be reinforced and Spellock was sealed in a stalemate. Outside, the army stood firm; inside, Loof pondered on what to do next.

The little Catchet flew to the top of the wall above the gates and stood gazing down at the enemy. He kept his balance while all around shook violently. He paused a moment, preparing a speech in his head, and then spoke.

'Baldore Mountain is angry at you. Can you feel its anger?' he asked them slyly. 'Hear what I say! If you persist in attacking my castle then I will kill all those I hold prisoner inside. If you leave peacefully I will let them go, but everyone will be under my command,' he said.

Sounds of protest came from the people, the Demonites and the Imps, but the Rock People made no sound. Loof wobbled slightly in the next violent tremor, but stood as still as he possibly could. He used his magic to lift himself up a few inches; to his audience he appeared rock solid.

'If you all leave I can make the mighty mountain calm and die, but if you continue *you* must all die.'

The three warlocks watched from the throne room, disgusted at the threat Loof was making to the crowds outside.

'Leave this place and never return!' A single voice lifted from the crowd and directed this statement at Loof. The Catchet looked down to see who had spoken.

'Who speaks and challenges me?' he questioned.

'I, Lord Faal of the Demonite people,' Faal answered.

'You have no authority here,' Loof boomed down at the Demonite.

'You have no right or authority in any part of this kingdom. Be gone from here,' the lone voice surged back.

'If you don't disperse immediately, I shall kill all the prisoners inside.' Loof's eyes were filled with rage and all the time the shuddering earth became more and more unstable.

Lord Faal whispered something to his underlings

and they, in turn, passed on the word. The Demonites murmured among themselves and soon began to move away from the walls of the castle. The Rock People also turned away, despite the protests of the people of Wizards' Kingdom. The Imps just look confused. Loof looked down and felt warmed by the satisfaction of victory that filled him.

A sound of thunder close by cracked across the cloudy expanse of sky. Baldore was heading for a huge eruption, but there was something else in the background, something moving through all the dust and haze. A steady *thud, thud, thud* rippled through the heavy rattle of the volcano's own rumblings. The thud changed to a mammoth clattering. Loof heard it and soon it caught everyone's attention.

In the distance the billowing, choking plumes of dust continued puffing into the atmosphere, leaving a veil of grey smoke settled on the landscape. The approaching figures emerged as mountainous shadows that slowly distinguished themselves from the gloom. Unsteadily, the shapes wobbled through the dusky blanket of dawn and strode across the land.

Loof stared curiously at first, with his beady black eyes. On closer inspection his stomach flipped and his evil eyes widened. The creatures penetrated the grey smoke and revealed themselves: trolls. Two hundred of them at least were heading straight for Spellock. There was only one person they were headed for and Loof knew it was him! He had killed Crockledam and they were out for revenge, but he still had his army and the power of the Orb. Inside him the evil welled up, making him feel strong and invincible. So, instead of relenting, he called his army to attack.

★

Zendal sat cross-legged on the floor to the side of the great throne with the Orb in front of him. Crasmont sat to his left side; he couldn't manage to cross his legs so he just sat awkwardly on his behind. To his left Mydar sat cross-legged, concentrating his stare on Zendal.

'There must be a way to enter the Orb and regain all our powers,' the old king said, turning his head to Crasmont.

'The problem we have, Zendal, is that we are not just dealing with Loof. We also have the task of trying to break the spell, if possible, that has given Jarrak his grip on Loof. We know how powerful he was before his demise and still is in his return,' the chubby wizard said, still trying to get comfortable on the floor.

'There is only one way we can do this, Master.' Mydar's voice sifted through from the darkness at the other side of the glass ball. All eyes turned towards him.

'Well…?' Zendal said, waiting for a response.

'We must contact the Elders and get their help,' Mydar said positively. Crasmont made immediate eye contact with Zendal. A smile filled the old warlock's face; he was clearly impressed.

'Well done, Mydar,' he expressed excitedly. 'How in Wizards' Kingdom did you think of that?' Zendal questioned.

'It's something you told me years ago, Master: that if all else failed and there were no alternatives, then calling the Elders would bring a solution to an impossible problem.'

'Yes… Yes I did, didn't I?' Zendal recalled as the screams of battle spilled in from outside and slabs of masonry broke away and fell around them.

'You also said there would be a penalty for calling the Elders, too. What did you mean by that, Master?' Mydar said, rubbing his chin.

'Don't worry about that now. We have no time to waste discussing this any further; this building will be a pile of rubble soon,' Zendal said urgently as he summoned his concentration.

'How do we do this, Zendal?' Crasmont asked curiously.

'There is only one way that I know and I've never done it before, but we must try,' Zendal said reluctantly.

Outside there was a pause in the sound of battle, but as the wizards began to attempt the connection, the full sound of war resumed.

'What do we do, Master?' Mydar asked, even though he had suggested the attempt.

'Everyone link hands and also touch the Orb,' Zendal instructed.

Zendal then touched one side of the Orb with his right hand. He gripped Crasmont's right hand with his left. Crasmont then gripped Mydar's right hand with his left and Mydar, in turn, placed his left palm on the other side of the Orb. A feeling of calm engulfed the room and the sound of battle stopped. Outside, things were very strange, very strange indeed. As if frozen in time, all the creatures involved in the fighting stood stock-still. The battle halted while the magic inside the throne room played out.

The wizards suddenly felt as though they were being sucked back to the very beginning of wizarding time. Their minds left the dark depression of war and took them on another journey. This time they were outside in the open air. The cities of the kingdom crumbled and fell. Forests grew larger and the sky beamed with brilliance. The landscape was moving, receding and changing. Zendal saw Lord Torsk and King Veltzeg reduced to little children, running and playing in the green lands and forests. Strange faces and voices rushed past in frenzy. Rulers of wizards and masters that history had only spoken of in half-remembered fables appeared and then were sucked away again. The sound of deep laughter, booming out to the point of cackling madness, consumed them. A rush of wind gusted in and lifted them high up onto the mountain. Abruptly, it all stopped!

Totally mystified by the incredible whirlwind of time they had witnessed, the wizards found themselves at the crown of Baldore Mountain, which was still a fearsome volcano. There, perched in the centre of the abyss, and suspended hundreds of feet above the heart of the bubbling, steaming lava, stood a temple of sorts – a huge, majestic and beautiful building. No path linked it to the volcano's rim. Standing on the volcano's outer edge, the wizards were held in awe at this incredible sight. Zendal, without any word to his companions, stepped forward. He felt an almost magnetic tug deep in his soul and couldn't hold back.

'Master, no!' Crasmont cried.

'It's all right, Crasmont… Just believe,' Zendal said calmly.

Mydar eased over to Crasmont and rested a hand on his shoulder, nodding as if he'd understood what Zendal was doing. Zendal took a few more steps until he, too, was suspended over the great crevasse. The others followed in turn, believing in Zendal's faith. A shudder shot through Crasmont's body, for each step took bundles of courage.

The wizards came to a stop outside the temple's entrance and they nervously entered. Inside, the building opened out into a colossal circular hall with a stone bench at the centre. A three-storey, half-moon-shaped bench overshadowed the proceedings. Still acting purely on instinct, the three wizards took seats in the body of the temple in front of the bench.

Seven hooded figures edged out of the darkness and

sat on the bench: two at the top, three in the middle and two more at the bottom. In the poor lighting of the ancient room the three wizards couldn't make out the Elders' features. Silence cloaked the hall for a few moments and the wizards waited patiently.

'Zendal.' A commanding voice rang out. 'Things are bad. Things are very bad.'

The other hooded figures surrounding the leader just nodded in agreement. There was silence once again.

'If I may, Your Lordship, we would not have called upon you for help and guidance if it were not a grave matter,' Zendal said humbly.

'We must put things right, Zendal, once and for all. So come forward,' the hooded Elder called out, motioning to Zendal with his hand. Crasmont and Mydar turned to one another and swallowed nervously.

Zendal approached the Elders and stood motionless. Murmurings were heard by the two wizards still seated, but they couldn't make out what was being said. From behind, they could see Zendal nodding. He then turned and walked back to his companions.

He looked his friends deep in the eyes and said, 'It is done.'

CLASH OF WIZARD AND CATCHET

'What is done, Master?' Mydar asked with urgency, but Zendal said no more.

Suddenly, everything around them became a blur. Rich colours shifted before their eyes as, once again, they travelled through the tunnel of wizard time. Before they knew it, they were back at Spellock, sitting around the Orb as if nothing had happened. Except Crasmont had noticed one change.

The clash of battle still engulfed everything around them, but he had seen something else.

'Zendal, have you noticed what's happened?' Crasmont said after standing up and peering outside.

'Yes, I know, my old friend,' Zendal replied.

'What do you mean? I can still hear all that was going on before we made the journey,' Mydar responded.

'Baldore Mountain, the volcano, has ceased, Mydar.' Crasmont turned and looked at his companion.

'What does that mean?' Mydar said, shaking his head in confusion.

'We have no time for explanations, Mydar, we have a battle to fight!' Zendal said, joining Crasmont at the window. The sight that greeted them was astounding. A colossal battle was in full swing.

Loof's army was pushing forward from the gates of

Spellock Castle. Thousands of winged and marching soldiers were clashing with every conceivable creature from the surrounding areas of Wizards' Kingdom: Rock People, Demonites, Imps and Wizards' Kingdom's own population. On the horizon, and moving in like a gigantic thunderstorm, were the trolls. Their mighty strength flattened the tyrants like scalding water poured over ants. They were scooping, crushing, tearing at and pummelling the enemy – an easy task for such a formidable force.

Mydar smiled broadly. 'Yes!' he shouted. Then his smile disappeared and turned to fear as, one by one, the almost invincible trolls began to tumble, smashing into the ground like fallen trees. As they fell, the wizard's could then see why.

Shafts of luminous-green light burst through the gloom of smoke and dust. Beams of energy impacted with troll after troll.

'Come on, let's finish this once and for all,' Zendal said and he leapt into the sky.

'What's happening?' Mydar's voice surged through the air from behind as he followed his master.

'It's Loof, Mydar. We must stop him before he finishes off our last hope of peace,' Crasmont shouted, as he too followed Zendal.

Loof caught a movement from the corner of his eye. He hastily broke off his attack and slipped away.

'Quickly, we're losing him!' Zendal hastened and quickly followed the slippery little creature. The Catchet soared parallel to the ground and cut across the fields, leaving the torment of battle well behind him. Close on his heels were the three wizards.

'Where's he going, Mydar?' Crasmont called from just above his companion.

Mydar looked up to his chubby companion, screwed up his face and shrugged his shoulders. His voice sounded calm at first, but he finished with a piercing shout: 'Crasmont... HOW SHOULD I KNOW?'

'Come on you two, there's no time for that,' Zendal shouted angrily.

The three wizards drew up level and saw the Catchet dip from sight into The Keep – a dense, dark wood where Crasmont and Mydar had once met Loof on their way to help Zendal rescue Shim from the Obelisk of Ashmar.

'Oh great! Just where we didn't need him to go,' Crasmont and Mydar uttered angrily in unison.

'Right, spread out. When you see him, call out, but don't take any chances. He's very dangerous now he's being followed,' Zendal ordered. Down into the depths the sorcerers dived, deep inside the mysteries of The Keep.

Each wizard landed in a different cold, dark place. Crasmont nervously darted his head around, searching. His heart was pounding so loudly he thought he'd give the game away. Twisted boughs, shaded in gloom, made it difficult to walk. Each step was taken carefully and silently.

Mydar moved on, casting his eyes in all directions. A deadly silence consumed the whole forest. A snapping branch stopped Mydar in his tracks. He strained his ears, closed his eyes and concentrated – something was close. He crouched behind a large tree stump and waited. His heart beat against his chest and his breathing became faster and more urgent; he could almost feel the blood surging through his veins. The shuffling came within range. He leapt out onto the mystery attacker, wrestling him to the ground.

'Crasmont!' Mydar burst out.

'Mydar, you idiot!' Crasmont bleated and they both sat up.

An enormous burst of light brought them to their senses and daylight filled the forest. They cupped their hands to shade their eyes.

'He's found him.' That was all Crasmont could say.

'Come on, let's help him.' Mydar had already got to his feet and was tearing through the brush like a demented Sharp Horn. To his amazement, The Keep's creatures were scampering towards him, but not to attack. They had fear in their eyes and were escaping past him.

As quickly as he could, Crasmont stood up and flew into the air, lifting himself high above the treetops. He could now travel as fast as his younger companion.

Mydar and Crasmont arrived at the source of the light at the same time. Loof and Zendal were locked in a power fight. On open ground the two were blasting energy into each other. Zendal's face was contorted in pain, but Loof wasn't smiling his usual victorious smile – his face, too, was twisted in agony. Crasmont landed by Mydar's side and both went to engage in the fight, but couldn't. The powerful connection between Zendal and Loof repelled the two wizards like opposing magnets. However hard they tried, they could not enter the ring of battle.

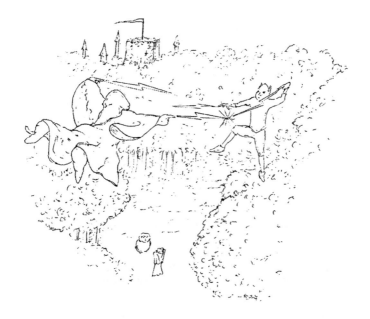

'What are we going to do, Crasmont?' Mydar cried through the sound of heavy, crackling energy.

'I don't think there's anything we can do, Mydar. I've never seen this amount of power before. I think it's more power than Zendal or Loof has ever had.' Crasmont turned to Mydar and gazed solemnly into his eyes.

'What is it, Crasmont?' Mydar asked with a tightening in his stomach.

'I'm not sure, but I think Zendal has the magic of the Elders and Loof has the power of Jarrak.'

'I... I don't understand,' Mydar stuttered.

'I think you do,' Crasmont replied. 'One must die; let's just hope it's the evil one.'

The fight went on and the atmosphere changed. Thunder sounded and lightning and black clouds appeared overhead. Rain and hail lashed down from the heavens and deafening rolls of thunder rocked the sky. Zendal and Loof's bodies lifted twenty feet off the ground with a gap between them of pure energy. Zendal's head tilted back; he opened his mouth wide and screamed. Satisfaction filled Loof's very soul and he emitted a sigh of relief.

'No... No... No!' Mydar cried, his eyes filling with tears.

Crasmont looked up with fear in his heart. From Loof's chest a dark shadow appeared. It seemed to be pulled from within the Catchet and wrenched out into the open. Its form evolved for a few moments and took the shape of Jarrak: black, evil and ugly. In the next few seconds it was pulled forwards relentlessly and sucked into Zendal's mouth; there it disappeared from sight. The bright flow of power instantly dimmed and died. The two bodies fell to the ground and lay still. Mydar and Crasmont rushed to Zendal's side and Mydar cradled his mentor in his arms. Zendal opened his eyes for a few moments and smiled.

'Master, Master, let us help you,' Mydar cried, pulling Zendal's head close to his chest.

'Zendal, what can we do?' The soothing voice of Crasmont flowed over Mydar's shoulder.

'There is nothing anyone can do, the Elders have spoken,' Zendal's answered in a calm voice.

'Don't die, Master. Please don't die.' Mydar wept and Crasmont gently squeezed his companion's shoulder.

'You will be king now and you must act as a king would. So weep no more – that's an order,' Zendal scolded with blazing eyes, but then their light dimmed and, slowly, they closed for ever.

★

Loof opened his eyes and sat up quickly. He felt strange and his body ached all over; his tired face winced with every movement. He looked around, taking in his surroundings. Startled, he stared in confusion at Mydar and Crasmont, both bent over on the ground. Loof rubbed his eyes and then caught sight of Zendal's limp body. A deep sadness immediately descended onto his heart like a heavy weight. *What has happened?* he thought.

Loof stood up and began to step forward to comfort his friends. A flicker of memory flashed across his confused mind – an evil, sickening memory that slammed into him like a sledgehammer. Slowly, he realised what Jarrak's power had done; what he had been forced to do while under the Catchet's wicked spell. He remembered everything – his own remorseless actions, although he had had no control over them. He stood with tears in his deep black eyes. He lowered his head in shame and turned to walk away.

Crasmont and Mydar looked up at Loof and could see the sorrow in his eyes. They could also see the old Loof, the friend that had helped them in the past. Now Jarrak was gone and Loof's goodness had returned.

The wizards beckoned to him to join them and he knelt at their side, mourning the death of the great King Zendal.

★

The battle came to an abrupt end. With the defeat of Jarrak's spirit, all the Seekers and Kites instantly disintegrated. A crack appeared in the sky, seeping a clear blue background. A deep yellow sun rose from the east, warming and melting the icy cold of winter, bringing in flocks of birds – a welcome sight after the domination of the Kites. Lush grass burst through the ground in a carpet of green.

Mydar, Crasmont and Loof gazed down as Zendal's body faded away into nothingness. He was gone, but now Wizards' Kingdom had a new king. Life was renewed as King Mydar began his rule.

Why not enjoy the first two books in the trilogy?

WIZARDS' KINGDOM

and

WIZARDS' KINGDOM: THE OBELISK OF ASHMAR

*M*EET THE *A*UTHOR

Colin R Parsons was born on 8 November 1960. He lives in the Rhondda Valley in the heart of South Wales, UK with his family. He has written the *Wizards' Kingdom* trilogy, which is popular with both children and adults.

He loves writing about fantasy, comedy and the 'unusual' and likes nothing more than to lose himself in another world.

Printed in the United Kingdom
by Lightning Source UK Ltd.
128572UK00001B/58-66/A